The Wicked Godmother

Also by Marion Chesney

The Wicked Godmother

Marion Chesney

St. Martin's Press / New York

Rom
Chesney

Library of Congress Cataloging in Publication Data

Chesney, Marion.
  The wicked godmother.

  (A House for the season ; 3rd)
  I. Title. II. Series: Chesney, Marion. House
for the season ; 3rd.
PR6053.H4535W5 1987   823'.914   86–26251
ISBN 0–312–00206–8

First Edition

10 9 8 7 6 5 4 3 2 1

For Rachael Feild
With love.

"Miss F.," says I, "is said to be
A sweet young woman, is not she?"
"O, excellent! I hear," she cried;
"O, truly so!" mamma replied.
"How old should you suppose her, pray?
She's older than she looks they say."
"Really," says I, "she seems to me
Not more than twenty-two or three."
"O, then you're wrong," says Mrs. G.
"Their upper servant told our Jane,
She'll not see twenty-nine again."
"Indeed, so old! I wonder why
She does not marry then," says I.

"Miss F.," says I, "I've understood,
Spends all her time in doing good;
The people say her coming down
Is quite a blessing to the town."
At that our hostess fetched a sigh,
And shook her head; and so, says I,
"It's very kind of her, I'm sure,
To be so generous to the poor."
"No doubt," says she, " 'tis very true;
Perhaps there may be *reasons* too:
You know some people like to pass
For *patrons* with the lower class."

And here I break my story's thread.
Just to remark, that what she said,
Although I took the other part,
Went like a cordial to my heart.

—JANE TAYLOR

Chapter
One

Gossip is mischievous, light and easy to raise, but
grievous to bear and hard to get rid of. No gossip
ever dies away entirely, if many people voice it; it
too is a kind of divinity.

—Hesiod

The sleepy little village of Upper Marcham had never before enjoyed such a
juicy scandal.

Widower and local worthy Sir Benjamin Hayner died
and left the management of his vast estates and all his
fortune to an impoverished gentlewoman, Harriet Metcalf.
Miss Metcalf was to hold control of said estates and fortune
until Sir Benjamin's twin daughters, Sarah and Annabelle,
should reach the age of twenty-one. The twins were only
eighteen years old. Harriet Metcalf, their godmother, was
a mere twenty-five years old.

Sir Benjamin had been a close friend of Harriet's parents and, after their death, had invited Harriet to dinner at
Chorley Hall, his stately residence, on many an occasion.

But no one, least of all his many relatives, expected
that he would will the control of his affairs to such a one as
Harriet.

1

The fact that she would have to surrender all on the twins' twenty-first birthday and return to living on a tiny income derived from a family trust did nothing to allay the pain.

For Harriet Metcalf was an Adventuress and a Scarlet Woman. After all, one had only to look at her.

She had a thick cloud of fluffy blond hair and huge deep blue eyes. She had thin arched eyebrows, which were quite dark, and long sooty eyelashes. Blondes were unfashionable. But that was not what made her suspect.

She had a willowy and seductive figure. She was of a sunny nature, but the locals and relatives claimed that no one with such an aura of strong sensuality could be anything other than No Better Than She Should Be. Sir Benjamin had been a handsome man. Tongues wagged as the villagers speculated on the nature of Miss Metcalf's relationship with the late Sir Benjamin Hayner.

Hitherto, Harriet had been respected and extremely popular.

One would have expected a certain amount of sour grapes on the part of the relatives, but the suspicions and animosity of the villagers were new, and Harriet was hurt and bewildered by it.

The fact was that all gossip stemmed from the twins themselves, who were so convinced, through their own jealousy of Harriet, that their stories were true that their scandals carried a ring of truth. Sarah and Annabelle were circumspect in their gossip, and no one ever quite knew the source of it—certainly not Harriet, who adored the twins and considered herself honoured that she was to have the care of them, if only for a short time. (Their birth had been too much for the late Lady Hayner, who had survived only a few hours after she had delivered them into the world.)

For Sir Benjamin had also requested in his will that Harriet should take the twins to London for their come-out, and if they failed to "take" at their first Season, then to present them at a second.

The funeral had been held on a bitterly cold December day, and Harriet had cried for at least two weeks afterwards. But desire to do the best for her old friend made her dry her eyes and begin to think about planning to take the girls to London.

Harriet lived in a cottage on the outskirts of the village. It was small, picturesque, Tudor, and damp. Up until her seventeenth year, she had lived with her parents in The Grange, a handsome Queen Anne mansion on the west side. Life had been comfortable; the future looked secure. It was understood Harriet would be taken to some genteel watering spa to make her come-out and there find a husband who was more interested in refinement than money. Mr. and Mrs. Metcalf prided themselves on their refinement. Mr. Metcalf often said the Metcalfs could have been dukes or earls had they not considered titles vulgar. Harriet never found their threadbare snobbery in the least odd. Never of a particularly critical disposition, Harriet loved and obeyed her parents and could not seem to understand why Sir Benjamin found their conversation, dress, and manners a constant source of amusement. The Metcalfs were more amusing than Astley's Amphitheatre, he used to say with his jolly laugh.

That his twin daughters disliked her and were jealous of her had never entered Harriet's innocent mind. She was too much in awe of her godchildren's exquisite gowns and accomplishments to see the spite beneath the correct facade.

After her parents' death, Harriet had been all too conscious of her straitened circumstances. Her parents had left many debts, and so the house and furniture had been sold, leaving only enough to allow Harriet to purchase the small cottage in which she now lived with Beauty, a large, slavering mongrel of tetchy disposition. Harriet loved Beauty: she often found humans erratic and puzzling, but felt safe with the devotion of this black-and-tan dog that loved her back while hating everyone else in the whole wide world.

There were very few members of the gentry in the village and certainly no female of Harriet's age whom her parents would have considered of suitable rank, and so when Sir Benjamin died, Harriet felt the need of a friend badly. Before the reading of the will, she had at least been on nodding terms with most of the village, but now, mysteriously, even the shopkeepers looked at her askance.

Any men who had proposed when her parents were alive had all been turned down by them as Quite Unsuitable, and now there seemed to be no man around who wanted to marry a spinster of twenty-five who did not even possess a dowry.

Harriet was, however, not entirely alone. An odd friendship had sprung up between the soft and lovely Harriet and a formidable spinster, of the parish of Upper Marcham, called Miss Josephine Spencer. But for the past two months Miss Spencer had been taking the waters in Bath, and, although Harriet had written to her, she had not received any reply.

She did not want to burden the twins with her troubles —they had surely enough to bear with the burden of their father's death. Much as she admired Sarah and Annabelle, Harriet could not help wishing the capricious knight had not seen fit to make her—at a ridiculously early age—the twins' godmother.

Harriet was sitting in the cold and bleak parlour of her cottage on a snowy afternoon, wondering what on earth to do next, when screams of fury coupled with loud barking and ending in the sound of ripping cloth came from the front garden.

It's Beauty, thought Harriet in dismay.

She ran and opened the low door of her cottage. There on the threshold, hammering Beauty on his thick narrow head with her umbrella, stood an irate Miss Josephine Spencer.

"Oh, Josephine," said Harriet, who was one of the very

few people who had ever been allowed to call Miss Spencer by her first name, "do come in. Down, Beauty! *Bad dog.*"

Beauty promptly rolled over on the path and stuck all four legs straight up in the air and managed not only to look like a dead dog but one in which rigor mortis had set in.

"Just look at my cloak," raged Miss Spencer. "A pox on that animal."

"I am so sorry," said Harriet, ushering her into the parlour. "See, your cloak has only parted at the seam, so if you will but give it to me, I shall have it mended in a trice."

Miss Spencer took off her cloak. "I don't know why you keep that dog. Useless for hunting, useless as a pet, vicious, greedy, and mean. If he were mine, I would shoot him! I say, you know I hate that beast. Haven't I always said so? Don't cry."

Harriet's blue eyes had filled with tears. "It is not that, Josephine," she sobbed. "I wish I had your strength. I feel so weak and silly."

"Compose yourself," said Josephine gruffly. "You know nothing really matters much if one has courage. Just look at me."

Harriet dried her eyes and surveyed her friend. No one could ever accuse Miss Spencer of weakness. She was a leathery woman with a sallow, lined face and small, twinkling black eyes. No one knew Miss Spencer's age, although she was believed to be in her fifties. She was wearing a repellent hard-hat and a gown of purple velvet, much seated. She had first met Harriet at a church fête three years ago. She did not know even now what had made her take such a liking to the younger woman, for Harriet was gentle and vague, and Miss Spencer normally found it very difficult to get along with members of her own sex at the best of times.

"Did you get my letter?" asked Harriet, taking a needle

5

and thread out of her workbasket and examining the seam of Miss Spencer's cloak. A dismal howl sounded from the garden. Beauty, thinking somewhere in the bony cavities of his limited brain that all must now be forgiven and forgotten, was demanding to be let in.

"Leave the horrible carriage rug where it is for the moment," said Miss Spencer. "Yes. I got your letter—eventually. Those Harrison people with whom I was staying assume that all correspondence consists of bills and so they simply stuffed it away along with all their unpaid accounts and did not discover it until a few days ago. I came as fast as I could. This is a very good piece of fortune. Very."

"How can you say that?" cried Harriet. "The poor twins have lost their father. I am to have the management of the estates and fortune and I have to bring the girls out and I don't even know where to begin."

"The good fortune is this. Until the girls are wed, you will be able to live in a comfortable style and have pretty gowns and a good London address, and, with luck, make a fine marriage for yourself."

"But I cannot afford clothes fine enough to allow me to act the part of a chaperone at the London Season."

"My dear child," said Miss Spencer, "you take the money out of the estate."

"I could not do that," said Harriet. "You see, after the reading of the will, Mrs. Draycott—you know, Sir Benjamin's sister—said in a very loud voice that she was sure I would contrive to feather my nest very nicely before the twins came of age. And also, the villagers are become most strange and unfriendly. I wondered whether Mrs. Draycott had set them against me."

"Mrs. Draycott, as you very well know, lives in the next county and never talks to anyone in the village here. Are you sure those two girls, Sarah and Annabelle, have not been gossiping nastily?"

"No!" exclaimed Harriet, much shocked. "Of course,

you do not know them at all well, but they are perfect ladies in everything they do, more mature than I and much more worldly. They would never stoop to do such a thing as gossip."

Miss Spencer delivered herself of a monumental sniff. Outside, Beauty set up another dismal howl. "I must let him in, dear Josephine," pleaded Harriet. "He will not touch you when you are in the room with me. You had been away so long, he had forgot you. He is not a very intelligent animal, but so good-hearted and my only friend apart from you so—"

"Let him in," said Miss Spencer grumpily, "and then perhaps we might be able to get down to business."

Harriet rushed from the room, and soon a volley of ecstatic yips and a scrabble of paws sounded from the tiny hall.

Beauty slouched in at Harriet's heels, waited until she was seated and settled with her sewing on her lap, and then he promptly lay down across her feet, turning one small, brown, bearlike, malevolent eye in Miss Spencer's direction. Miss Spencer glanced around the parlour and thought, not for the first time, that all men were fools. It was so like a man, so like the late Sir Benjamin, carelessly to leave such a dotty will. How much more sensible it would have been to have left poor Harriet a tidy sum and thereby ensured her independence.

The parlour was as pretty as Harriet with her straitened means could contrive to make it. A decorative spray of autumn leaves, preserved in glycerine, glowed from a bronze jug in the shadows of the candlelit room. There were two elegant Sheraton chairs and a pretty inlaid table, but the uneven floor was bare and the fireplace a very cottagey sort of arrangement full of dark hooks and chains, showing it had been used for cooking in the days before the tiny kitchen extension had been added.

"You were going to talk about business," prompted

Harriet gently. She was already feeling much recovered. There was something very reassuring about Miss Spencer's no-nonsense approach to life.

"The first thing we need to do is to go to see Sir Benjamin's lawyer," said Miss Spencer. "He will arrange for you to be paid a sufficient sum out of the estate to enable you to chaperone and present the girls in style. He will also be able to rent a house for you for the Season. He may find it a little difficult to get you a tonnish address, but he must try. You should not be staying here. As the girls' godmother and duenna, you should be in residence at Chorley Hall."

"I felt that might be a little presumptuous," said Harriet.

"Yes, you *would,*" said Miss Spencer. "It is too late to worry about that now. The one move you should be thinking of making is to London. You will need to be there as soon before the Season begins as possible. You must nurse the ground—that is, give little tea parties, get to know the women of the ton, particularly any women with sons of a marriageable age."

"It is all rather daunting," said Harriet. "I do not know much about the world."

"No, nor people either," said Miss Spencer.

She spoke sharply, and Beauty stirred at Harriet's feet, curling back his black lips in a snarl.

"I mean," went on Miss Spencer, eyeing Beauty with dislike but carefully moderating her tone of voice, "you do not know the Hayner girls very well. I know you are about to say that is ridiculous, but only think! You never actually played with them when you were all little girls together. You have only seen them in Sir Benjamin's company. I have heard it said they take after the mother, who was a cunning shrew."

"Josephine," said Harriet, turning pink, "I have long admired both Sarah and Annabelle. They have a niceness, a delicacy, and refinement, which I must confess I find lacking in myself. Their social manners are faultless. I am shy and never can think what to say to people. They have always welcomed me and were extremely kind and sympathetic when my parents died."

"They used to call on you when you lived at The Grange," said Miss Spencer. "How many times have they called since you moved here?"

"What has come over you, Josephine?" said Harriet reproachfully. Then her face cleared. "I know why you are so tetchy. It is the fatigue of the long journey, and, besides, we have discussed only my troubles and said never a word about your experiences in Bath. Do tell me about all the people who were there? Did the waters help your spleen?"

Miss Spencer, realising gloomily that Harriet's loyalty to the Hayner twins was apparently unshakeable, settled down to entertain her young hostess with an acid description of Bath society out of season.

Harriet sat and listened while finishing mending the tear in Miss Spencer's cloak, glad that her friend had at least stopped criticising the twins.

At that very moment, half a mile to the north of Upper Marcham, Sarah and Annabelle were arriving home to Chorley Hall after a futile visit to their father's lawyer in the county town of Barminster.

They stood in the hall, removing their cloaks and listening to the hum of conversation coming from the small saloon on the ground floor. Sir Benjamin's sister-in-law, Miss Giles, had taken up residence after the funeral and showed no signs of leaving. Neither did his brother, Mr. Peter Hayner, nor his brother's wife, Mrs. Amy Hayner.

"I cannot bear any of them at this moment," said Sarah. "Let us go to the upstairs drawing room, Annabelle. We must hold a council of war." She turned to the butler. "Biggins, don't you dare tell any of them we have returned." She put her arm around her sister's waist and together they mounted the broad oaken staircase.

"Now, what on earth are we to do about that tiresome Harriet creature?" said Sarah, pushing open the door of the drawing room. "Throw another log on the fire, Annabelle, and don't always be ringing the bell for the servants to do everything or we shall never have a chance of a private discussion."

"The servants are paid to do things," grumbled Annabelle, but she was too lazy ever to argue much with her stronger-willed sister.

The Hayner twins might have been exactly alike had not their somewhat different characters moulded their appearances. Sarah was thin and energetic and Annabelle plump and languid. Sarah was always very intense about everything, while Annabelle faced most of life's vicissitudes with only an occasional grumble. She had become used to allowing Sarah to deal with all problems. In the presence of company, their likeness to each other was more marked, as both affected the same social manner—a sort of decorous femininity that involved many suppressed giggles, fan flutterings, rolling eyes, and conversations confined to the most trivial topics. In fact, they went on very much as debutantes of good breeding were expected to do. Had they been of a lesser caste, then they would not have been considered very pretty, but a great deal of money added a lustre to their appearance in the eye of any beholder less cynical than, say, Miss Josephine Spencer.

Both had thick brown hair, fashionably dressed; both had straight little noses and tiny, pouting, rosebud mouths. But both were inclined to be sallow. They wore pastel colours that did not flatter them, and the high-waisted modes hung loosely on Sarah's thin figure and showed Annabelle's plump figure to disadvantage, in the latter case mainly because she wore her gown cut too narrow and too tight.

They had just learned—again—from the lawyer, Mr. Gladstone, that the terms of the will were all too clear. They were to be brought out in London by Miss Harriet Metcalf, and there was nothing to be done about it. In vain had Sarah raged that Harriet was a schemer who had bewitched their father and that she would use up their fortune and leave them naught. Mr. Gladstone had said firmly that Sir Benjamin's opinion was that Miss Metcalf was the only honest woman left in Britain—an opinion, said Mr. Gladstone, that he himself shared. The handling and running of the estates would be carried on as it had been in Sir Benjamin's lifetime by his agent, Robert Wyckoff. Mr. Wyckoff would, of course, consult Miss Metcalf on all matters. Sarah then said that Miss Metcalf had no connections and was a country bumpkin and was not a fitting person to chaperone them at the London Season. Mr. Gladstone replied unsympathetically that he was sure Miss Metcalf would do her best, and if the Misses Hayner thought they could do better, they had only to wait until they were twenty-one.

"Do you think, as we cannot legally do anything at all about Harriet," ventured Annabelle, "that it might not be wiser just to let her take us to London?"

"And watch her fleece us?" demanded Sarah.

"I do not like her either, Sis," said Annabelle. "But, do you know, I doubt if the silly little widgeon will take a penny more than is due to her. After all, she is not the sweet innocent she tries to make everyone believe she is. She did take Papa's affection away from us. You know she did."

"And she shall be made to suffer for it," said Sarah, spreading her thin hands out over the blaze. "You do sometimes have good ideas, Annabelle. Let us go to London. We are both pretty enough to rival the Gunter sisters. We shall both probably be engaged by the end of the Season."

"Do not compare us to the Gunter sisters," giggled Annabelle. The Gunter sisters had been famous in the last century for their dazzling marriages. "Do you know what one of them is supposed to have said to George II? The old king was complaining he did not like public displays, and one of the Misses Gunter said blithely, 'Neither do I, Your Majesty. The only public display I wish to see is the next coronation!'"

Sarah collapsed in helpless giggles. Finally, she dried her streaming eyes and said, "We must make sure that Harriet does not lure the gentlemen's eyes away from us with her sneaky ways. Look how she made Papa love her as a daughter, and that is what I cannot forgive. Had she flirted with him and made him look upon her as a possible mistress, that I could have borne. But to sit there with her empty blue eyes, pretending to be Saint Thingummy was sickening to watch."

"And Papa would not hear one word against her."

"But just wait until we get you to London, Miss Harriet Metcalf, and there you will see that your innocent, countrified ways are considered a bore." She pretended to raise a quizzing glass to her eye and stared haughtily at Annabelle. *Pon rep,*" said Sarah in a deep voice, "who is that preposterous milkmaid of a gal with the beautiful Hayner twins?"

"It's really all too deliciously funny," said Annabelle, beginning to giggle again. Sarah aimed a playful punch at her, and then both sisters rolled about the sofa, helpless with laughter at the thought of the comeuppance of Miss Metcalf.

Harriet and Miss Spencer were leaving Harriet's cottage on the following day to pay a visit to the lawyer, Mr. Gladstone, when that gentleman surprised them by appearing at the garden gate. Glad to be saved a journey to Barminster, the ladies ushered him into the cottage parlour, where Harriet poured out her troubles. Mr. Gladstone was all that was reassuring. The estates' business matters would be handled as they had always been handled; money matters would be taken care of by himself. Harriet should be paid an allowance until such time as the twins came of age. As to finding a house for the Season? Mr. Gladstone smiled triumphantly and produced a crumpled copy of the *Morning Post* out of one capacious pocket.

"I have taken the liberty of answering an advertisement in this newspaper," he said. "The house advertised is a good address, and the price is very reasonable."

He pointed to an advertisement on the front of the newspaper.

Harriet and Miss Spencer leaned forward. They read,

A HOUSE FOR THE SEASON
Gentleman's residence, 67
Clarges Street, Mayfair.
Furnished town house. Trained
servants, Rent: £80 sterling.
Apply, Mr. Palmer, 25 Holborn.

"Wonderful!" said Harriet.

"Too cheap for such a tonnish address," said Miss Spencer with a worried frown. "I wonder if there is anything wrong with it."

Chapter Two

The rain it raineth on the just
And also on the unjust fella;
But chiefly on the just, because
The unjust steals the just's umbrella.

—Charles, Baron Bowen

It had been raining for weeks and weeks. Rain chuckled in the gutters and ran in streams in the kennels in the middle of the London streets. Rain pounded down with merciless democracy on the slums of Seven Dials and the quiet streets of Mayfair.

A government lottery sledge scraped its way along Clarges Street, and the resultant wave from its progress sent a miniature Niagara Falls tumbling down the area steps of Number 67 Clarges Street and sent a tide of muddy water dashing over the white silk stockings of the footman, Joseph, who opened the door just in time to receive the full benefit of the flood. He let out a squawk like an outraged parrot and retreated back through the kitchen and into the servants' hall.

"Look at meh stockings," he screeched. "Bleck as pitch."

"Go and change," said the butler, Rainbird, testily. "It's not the end of the world."

But Joseph—tall, fair, effeminate, and vain—would not be comforted. "It is the end of the world," he said mournfully, sitting down at the table next to Rainbird, removing one buckled shoe and emptying the water from it out onto the kitchen floor, then taking off one stocking, and then studying his own naked foot with surprise as if he had never really noticed it before. "Eh hehve never known such rain," went on Joseph in accents of strangulated gentility. "Rain, rain, rain, and no tenant for the Season."

"As to that," said Rainbird cautiously, "I received a note from Jonas Palmer saying he would call on us today. Mayhap he has some good news for us."

Several pairs of hopeful eyes turned in his direction. The staff of Number 67 had just finished breakfast. Apart from Joseph and Rainbird, seated round the table were the Highland cook, Angus MacGregor; Mrs. Middleton, the housekeeper; Jenny, the chambermaid; Alice, the housemaid; little Lizzie, the scullery maid; and Dave, the pot boy. They were an oddly assorted group of people, welded into a closely knit clan, or family, by peculiar circumstances.

Number 67 Clarges Street was still damned as unlucky. It was owned by the tenth Duke of Pelham, the ninth duke having hanged himself there. Although Number 67 had managed to find tenants for the past two Seasons, the dramatic happenings which had occurred to them while living there had made the polite world wary of choosing it as a town residence. Palmer, the agent, paid the servants rock-bottom wages, while charging his young master higher ones. He had collected unsavoury facts about Rainbird and Joseph and threatened to ruin them should they try to leave. The hold he had had on the others was simply that he would not give them references. Jobs in London were impossible to find without a reference, and scarce enough even if one had one. The previous tenant, the new Lady Tregarthan, had supplied the staff with glowing references, but they knew that no household would take them en masse. They had become so close, they were reluctant to part and dreamed instead of saving enough money so that they could buy a pub and run it as a joint effort.

Rainbird was the "father" of the family. He was a well-set up man in his forties, with a wiry acrobat's body and a comedian's face. Mrs. Middleton—the "Mrs." was a courtesy title—was the daughter of a curate who had fallen on hard times. She was, as the French so delicately put it, a lady of certain years, with a face like a frightened rabbit, which was mostly overshadowed by the huge starched frills of the caps she liked to wear. The cook, MacGregor, was Highland, emotional, and had a temper to match his shock of fiery red hair. Jenny was quick and dark, with brisk, nervous movements. In contrast to the chambermaid, Alice, the housemaid, was blond and Junoesque, with slow, languid movements and a voice like rich Cornish cream. Little Lizzie, less waiflike than she had first been when she had entered service, had a pale face, thick nut-brown hair, and the large trusting eyes of a puppy. She was seated next to Joseph, instead of down at the end of the table where she belonged—but the servants rarely observed their caste system when the house was untenanted. Although only the scullery maid, she was treated with a certain amount of rough affection by the others. Dave, the pot boy, was a wizened little Cockney. He was only fourteen, but his early years as a chimney sweep's apprentice had stunted his growth and aged his face.

All hated Jonas Palmer, the Duke of Pelham's agent, although they did not know that the young duke, who owned a larger town house in Grosvenor Square, was unaware of their existence. They had heard the duke had finished his studies at Oxford University and had gone to the Peninsula to fight Napolean's troops.

Despite the fact that all had ended happily for the previous tenants of the past two Seasons after their adventures, the house could not seem to lose its name for being unlucky, and during this age when gambling fever was at a height and superstition rampant, the future of its staff remained uncertain. The Duke of Pelham had hanged himself there, and that seemed enough to put a curse on the place, which all went to show the power of the class system. Servants committed suicide with amazing regularity, but their parting with the world did not put their masters' town residence into bad odour. But a duke committing suicide—ah, well, that was an entirely different thing.

The servants depended on a successful Season as much, if not more, than any matchmaking mama. Because of their abysmally low wages, they looked forward to the tips they would gain from the Season's festivities.

Rainbird rose to his feet. "We had best make sure this place is spotless before Palmer comes," he said. "It would serve you better, Joseph, if you put your back into your work instead of paddling out on the street."

"I didn't even get as far as the street," whined Joseph, his basic Cockney vowels creeping back into his genteel accent like blobs of grease surfacing on a pot of soup. "I jest opened the bleeding door and got hit by a wave."

"Why did you not say so!" exclaimed Mrs. Middleton. "Dave, you get the floor rag and help Lizzie clean up the mess. Jenny and Alice, come with me. We had best light the fire in the front parlour." The two maids followed the housekeeper upstairs.

It was a typical town house of the period, being tall and thin. On the ground floor there was a hall with a drawing room to one side, consisting of front and back parlours. On the first floor, there was the dining room, with a double bedroom at the back. On the second floor, there were two bedrooms, and then there were the attics at the top where the servants slept, with the exception of Lizzie and Dave. Lizzie bedded down in the scullery, and Dave slept under the kitchen table.

There was a ghostly air about the rooms where all the furniture was shrouded in holland covers and all the clocks stood silent, as if time out of Season did not count, as if the hours waited only for the return of all the noise and glitter, gossip and broken hearts, that another fashionable London Season would bring.

Jenny and Alice bundled the holland covers off the chairs in the front parlour. "At least we haven't taken any stuffing out of these seats," said Jenny. The servants had, in the past, often augmented their meagre income by removing the stuffing from the beds and upholstery and selling it, so that you could always gauge the hardness of the times at Number 67 by the discomfort you had when either sitting or lying down. Last Season had been very profitable, and, for once, they had all passed a tolerable winter. But funds were beginning to run low.

Joseph had become convinced last October that Prime 'Un would win at Newmarket races and had talked everyone but Rainbird and Mrs. Middleton into letting him put most of their savings on the wonderful horse. But the horse had fallen on its nose halfway down the course, and so the furious butler and housekeeper had had to use up their savings on keeping the rest of the ashamed and destitute staff warm and fed.

Rain trickled down the windowpanes as Jenny and Alice dusted and polished. "It is cold in here," said Mrs. Middleton. "I shall fetch Joseph to make up the fire and wind the clocks. You know Mr. Palmer expects us to be prepared to receive people at all times."

Soon a fire was crackling on the hearth, and the clocks were busily ticking away, bringing with their chatter and chimes a feeling of expectancy. Time had returned to Number 67 Clarges Street. All that was now needed was a tenant.

Jonas Palmer arrived an hour early, hoping to catch them unprepared, but Rainbird was used to the agent's ways and had made sure everyone was ready at least three hours before his expected arrival.

18

"Where's Alice?" demanded Palmer, glaring with his bulging eyes at Jenny, who was setting the tea tray on a table in the front parlour.

"Alice is out on an errand," said Rainbird. The butler did not like the way the agent always leered at the beautiful Alice and undressed her with his eyes, and so he had told the housemaid to stay belowstairs. Jenny left the room, and Rainbird looked expectantly at the agent.

"Do well for yourself, you lot," said Palmer grumpily, stretching his thick legs out towards the fire and glancing around the well-kept parlour. Rainbird waited patiently. It was useless to argue with Palmer.

Palmer slurped his tea noisily. It was amazing, reflected Rainbird, how the agent could manage to drink a cup of tea with the spoon still sticking in it and not jab himself in the eye.

"I spoke to his grace t'other day," said Palmer, "and he said to me, he says, them servants at Sixty-seven are too highly paid."

Rainbird looked at Palmer, his grey eyes suddenly sharp with suspicion. "Does the Duke of Pelham actually know what we are being paid?"

" 'Course he does. Don't I take the books to him regular?"

"And how was it in the Peninsula?" asked Rainbird sweetly. "Hot?"

"What?"

"The Duke of Pelham has been in Portugal since last summer, so if you were speaking to him, I assume you plodded over the high mountains in order to achieve that end."

"Don't take that hoity-toity tone with me," growled Palmer, turning red. "You're nothing but a womaniser who wouldn't have no pay at all if it weren't for me."

Rainbird had been dismissed from Lord Trumping- ton's household for having been found between the sheets with a very naked Lady Trumpington. The fact that my lady had practically dragged him into bed was not taken into account. Rainbird was dismissed in disgrace and, had it not been for Palmer, would have found it very hard to get another post, as Lord Trumpington had called him a mad rapist to anyone who would listen.

Servants were always wrong. It was the custom for a man of society to take his footman along when he dined from home. The footman's job was to pick his master up from under the table at the end of the meal and manage to get him home without occasioning any Methodist remarks about drunkenness. But should the master behave so badly that his far-gone inebriated state was impossible to conceal, as in the case of a certain lord who insisted on performing *entrechats* in the middle of the dining table, then it was the footman who was accused of drunkenness and dismissed.

Rainbird remained silent. He felt sure if he managed to wait quietly long enough then the agent would get around to talking about the real purpose of his visit.

And so it was. After trying unsuccessfully to bait Rainbird, Palmer heaved a disappointed sigh and said, "A tenant is arriving next month. Parcel of women, by the looks of it. Saw the lawyer concerned. Seems this knight, Sir Benjamin Hayner, died and left his two daughters in the care of a twenty-five-year-old miss called Metcalf. This Miss Metcalf will be arriving with the two girls. Again, there is going to be the question of accommodation for their lady's maid."

Rainbird winced, and Palmer looked at him curiously. Rainbird had fallen in love with the French lady's maid who had been resident the last Season.

"Last year," said Rainbird, carefully controlling his expression, "Mrs. Middleton had to give up her parlour on the backstairs. I trust this won't be necessary again."

"It's all up to this Metcalf. Leave it to her. She should be something new in your experience, Rainbird. According to this lawyer, she's the biggest saint in the length and breadth of England."

"Good," said Rainbird. "A saintly tenant would care for the welfare of the servants. In fact, any *lady* cares for her servants. It is only those who are neither ladies nor gentlemen who treat servants badly."

"Meaning me," said Palmer, a dangerous colour mounting up his face.

Rainbird studied him with the curiosity of a jackdaw, as if hoping the terrible Palmer might have an apoplexy and leave this world a better place, but Palmer soon recovered and demanded to see the housekeeping accounts.

At long last the ordeal was over. Mrs. Middleton took the books back to her parlour and comforted herself with a good cry, for Palmer's rude and brutal manner always made her feel as if she had been assaulted. She dried her eyes and looked up as Rainbird entered the room.

"Oh, Mr. Rainbird," she said, fluttering to her feet. "I am afraid I have been crying, and my eyes are so red and . . ."

"It does not matter," said Rainbird. "I brought a little brandy to comfort both of us. I know we should share it with the others, but then, they are not so much in need of comfort at the moment as we. How that wretched man does rile me! Also, *we* did not lose our well-earned money on some useless horse."

"I suppose they cannot be blamed all the same," said the housekeeper. "Joseph made the bet sound so tempting —and I would have certainly given him my money if you had not been so much against it, Mr. Rainbird. We cannot all be as clever as you." She sighed and gazed at him adoringly, but the butler was busy pouring the brandy and did not notice her doting expression.

"Now, Mrs. Middleton," said Rainbird, settling down in a battered armchair opposite the housekeeper, "things look quite hopeful for the coming Season. Palmer said a

Miss Metcalf is the new tenant. She is quite young, but she is to chaperone two young misses during their debut. According to the new tenant's lawyer, this Miss Metcalf is a sort of saint. I shall ask her to raise our wages for the term of the rental, only to the level we should be getting paid. They are bringing a lady's maid. . . ."

Mrs. Middleton looked miserable again. The last lady's maid had not only taken up residence in the housekeeper's parlour but had stolen Rainbird's heart. "As far as I can gather," went on Rainbird gently, "this lady's maid might be well-content to share a room with Alice and Jenny."

"Well, it will be nice," said Mrs. Middleton cautiously, "to have only ladies in the house. They are so much easier to look after than the gentlemen, saving your presence, Mr. Rainbird. Yes, young ladies will be a pleasant change."

Miss Josephine Spencer stood in the rain with a large silk umbrella over her head, watching the Misses Hayner and Harriet preparing to leave Chorley House. She herself had conveyed Harriet, Beauty, and Harriet's shabby trunks by her own gig from the village.

She had had some conversation with the twins before they had left the house and was relieved to find their manner towards Harriet affectionate. Nothing to worry about there.

But it appeared as if the girls had suddenly discovered that Beauty was also going to London.

"You cannot possibly take that mongrel into society," giggled Sarah. "Give the cur to Miss Spencer. I am sure she will look after him for you."

Harriet looked embarrassed. "I am sorry, Sarah, but I must insist he comes. I shall keep him away from you. He is such a good watchdog."

"Stoopid," said Annabelle. "You do not understand, dear Harriet. The dog stays behind."

"I must insist," said Harriet, who had fed Beauty a

large meal so that the animal might look more placid and approachable than usual.

"Then, if you insist, it may go in the baggage coach with Emily." Emily was the twins' lady's maid. Miss Spencer looked curiously at Emily. She thought Emily looked like a fox with her reddish-brown hair and eyes of a peculiar shade of yellow. Emily gave her mistresses a sidelong look, and then her thin mouth curled in a faint grimace.

"I do not think that a very good idea," said Harriet. "I—"

Beauty suddenly bared his teeth and gave the twins a sinister canine sneer. He growled far back in his throat, a threatening rumble.

"Oh, very well, Harriet," said Sarah. "But it is most odd of you."

"Thank you," said Harriet with a sunny smile. A footman was holding open the carriage door. Harriet urged Beauty in and then climbed in after the dog.

It was then that Miss Spencer saw Sarah turn to Annabelle and roll her eyes heavenwards in mock resignation. Then she went through the mime of wringing someone's neck. Annabelle laughed hysterically, and then they both got into the coach after Harriet.

Miss Spencer shook her head as if to clear it. It was natural that anyone would be annoyed with Harriet for insisting the dog went along as well. The animal was quite horrible. On the other hand, she knew the girls had for the moment forgotten her presence, and the air of contempt and dislike exuding from the two of them had been almost tangible.

Miss Spencer walked to the carriage window. Harriet was sitting with her back to the horses and Beauty was lying at her feet.

"Good-bye, Harriet," said Miss Spencer. "If you are in need of help, write to me and I shall come to London directly."

"Good-bye, Josephine," said Harriet, looking at her friend through a blur of tears. "I am sure I shall not be in need of help, but, of course, I shall write to you just the same."

"Good-bye, Miss Spencer," chorused the twins, looking the very pattern cards of propriety.

Miss Spencer stood back, her fears put to rest. The twins were very pleasant little girls. She had been imagining things.

The coachman cracked his whip; the carriage began to roll off down the drive. Harriet's lace handkerchief fluttered briefly at the window. The coach passed the lodge gates and swung out onto the London road.

Miss Spencer climbed into her own gig and picked up the reins. Life seemed empty and flat. Miss Spencer began to run through in her mind the names and addresses of all her friends and relatives in London. Perhaps she might go on a visit, just to see Harriet's coming out.

For it was Harriet's debut as much as it was the twins'.

Chapter
Three

There pay it, James! 'tis cheaply earned;
My conscience! how one's cabman charges!
But never mind, so I'm returned
Safe to my native street of Clarges.

—H.D. Traill

At first it seemed as if Number 67 was all set for one of the most tranquil periods the town house had known since it was first built early in the previous century.

From Rainbird down to Dave, the staff vowed they had never known such sweet and charming ladies.

Miss Metcalf, on being appealed to by Rainbird shortly after her arrival for an increase in the staff's wages, had said she would write to the lawyer, Mr. Gladstone, asking his permission. Mr. Gladstone had replied that since the servants appeared to be asking only a reasonable amount, he would allow Harriet to pay the increase, but added that he had written to Mr. Palmer, complaining that servants should be paid so little in this year of Our Lord, 1809.

At first Harriet was at a loss as to how to begin finding suitable social company for her charges, but Rainbird had stepped in with a list of the correct people to cultivate.

Joseph was sent to the pub patronised by the upper servants, The Running Footman, to spread the gossip that the Hayner girls were very rich, and soon a few invitation cards began to arrive.

London was still thin of company, but Harriet was anxious to give Sarah and Annabelle a head start on the other hopeful debutantes.

Much of the day was taken up being pinned and fitted by the dressmaker. Sarah and Annabelle were furious when it transpired that Harriet was to have a new wardrobe as well, but they concealed their rage, writing instead to Mr. Gladstone, demanding such extravagance on the part of their godmother be stopped. Mr. Gladstone replied that it was only right that Harriet should be decked out in a style that befitted her station and it would shame the Misses Hayner in the eyes of the ton were they to appear with a poorly dressed chaperone.

To do them justice, the twins had become firmly convinced some time ago that Harriet had stolen away their father's affection. But the sad fact was that Sir Benjamin had come to despise and dislike his vindictive wife during her lifetime. After seeing too many of her nastier traits in his own daughters, which no teaching by several excellent governesses could appear to eradicate, Sir Benjamin had come to the conclusion that both his daughters were sly and devious. But he was a careless and jovial man, not given to much deep thought on any subject. He was rarely at home, and, when he was, he always summoned Harriet to dinner —a practise that his daughters had hoped would end with the death of Harriet's parents. Up until then, they had thought Papa merely amused at the foibles of the shabby-genteel Metcalfs, and it was only after the death of Mr. and Mrs. Metcalf that his real affection for Harriet began to shine through. They had always concealed their envy and dislike of Harriet very well, and Sir Benjamin would never have saddled Harriet Metcalf with his daughters' debut had he guessed the extent of their jealousy.

But the early days, while the girls prepared for the Season, passed pleasantly enough. By rigorous dieting, Annabelle had managed to lose a few pounds of weight, and by eating regular meals, Sarah had gained the same amount of weight her sister had lost. They came to look very alike, although Sarah was still nervous and intense and Annabelle sluggish and lazy.

Both agreed privately that Harriet should be treated with courtesy until she had created the groundwork for their social success. That she worked so hard at achieving this end did nothing to soften the feeling of either towards her.

Perhaps the only person in the house who was not very happy was Lizzie, the scullery maid. Try as she would, she could not like Emily, the lady's maid. Emily had not ousted Mrs. Middleton from her parlour, but appeared content to share an attic with Jenny and Alice. Nor had Emily caught Joseph's eye, something that really would have annoyed Lizzie, who was hopelessly in love with the vain footman. It was that Lizzie sensed a cruelty in Emily which the others did not seem to notice. She had a secretive way of looking at people out of the corners of those odd yellow eyes of hers, as if she was privately laughing at some particularly nasty joke.

And Lizzie was, moreover, not feeling very well. The rain still poured down, day after day, which meant muddied floors and floods in the kitchen to clean up. There were also fires to be made up in all the rooms and fenders to be polished.

All the servants had eyed Beauty askance, particularly Joseph, who was not only frightened it would savage his pet —the kitchen cat called the Moocher, a tawny, disreputable miniature lion of an animal—but was also dismayed to learn he was expected to take the beast out for walks.

But Beauty created no problems. He trudged miserably at Joseph's heels outdoors and slept in front of the fire indoors. Harriet thought her pet was adapting well to city life, mainly because she had not very much time to worry about his oddly chastened mood. But the truth of the matter was that Beauty had cankers in his ears and was in perpetual pain and discomfort. His coat grew shabby and dull, and he barely touched his food.

An end came to the dog's misery one day when Joseph was walking him along Curzon Street. A light carriage had overturned, spilling its occupants into the kennel. Joseph stopped to watch the drama. Then he found he was being addressed by a tall, elegant gentleman.

"Is that your dog?" asked the gentleman. Joseph looked up—it was not often that Joseph, who was tall, had to look up at anyone—and saw a strong, handsome face shadowed by the brim of a beaver hat.

"No," said Joseph, who was ashamed of Beauty's mangy looks. "Belongs to my mistress."

"It looks ill," said the tall gentleman. He bent down to where Beauty sat shivering in the rain at the side of the pavement, looked at the dog's teeth, and then flipped back Beauty's floppy ears, one after the other.

He straightened up. "The dog has cankers in both ears. Give me your direction, and I shall leave a solution with your mistress that will cure the animal of his discomfort in a few days."

Joseph, who had already taken in the richness of the gentleman's clothes, said promptly, "Number Sixty-seven Clarges Street. Miss Metcalf."

"Here is my card," said the gentleman.

Joseph took it and read the name, THE MARQUESS OF HUNTINGDON. His eyes widened. Joseph knew all the gossip there was to know about his betters. The marquess, he remembered, had been abroad for a long time in America, where he owned a tobacco plantation in Virginia. He was reputed to be one of the richest men in England, and the most handsome.

"Yes, my lord," he said, bowing so low he almost

touched noses with Beauty. The marquess nodded and strolled off along Curzon Street with his friend, Lord Vere.

"Why on earth did you waste your time over that brute of a dog?" said Lord Vere. "There's nothing up with it that a good bullet straight between the eyes wouldn't mend."

"I noticed it looked sick," said the marquess mildly. "But you are quite right. I should curb these charitable impulses. Now I have to call on some old spinster called Metcalf at Number Sixty-seven Clarges Street and give her medicine for the brute. But it's good stuff. I've used it on my own hounds, and if it can put one more animal out of misery, then why not?"

"I'll come with you," said Lord Vere eagerly. "When are you going?"

"Possibly tomorrow. Why so eager to accompany me?"

"Vulgar curiosity, that's why. I want to get a look at the inside of that famous Clarges Street town house and see the sort of lady who's brave enough to take it."

"What is so special about the house? Is it haunted?"

"In a way. There's a curse on it. All sorts of odd things happen to people who stay there. The old Duke of Pelham hanged himself there. The house now belongs to the new duke, but he never goes near it. It's the place where Clara Vere-Baxton died and last Season the new Lady Tregarthan discovered Clara had been murdered by Dr. Gillespie."

"Oh, I remember that scandal," said the marquess. "But you surely don't believe in all that fustian about a curse. Come with me tomorrow, and we shall find, I assure you, some sweet little old lady, no doubt short-sighted, who does not even know her dog is sick."

Joseph presented the marquess's card to Harriet when he returned. The twins were out shopping with their maid, Emily. Harriet was too shocked upon finding out her pet was ill to pay much attention to the fact that it was a marquess who was going to supply the cure. She told Joseph to fetch her a bowl of potassium permanganate and warm water and some cotton wool.

Then she knelt down beside Beauty and gently lifted his ears, wincing as she saw the angry scarlet infection inside. She gently bathed his ears, fussing over him, and he rolled his eyes miserably and feebly licked her hand.

So ashamed was Harriet that she had not noticed how ill her dog was that she failed to tell the girls about the Marquess of Huntingdon. Also, she knew that Sarah and Annabelle did not like Beauty. Had Joseph told her that the marquess was an eligible and handsome man, then she would most certainly have roused the twins early in the morning to prepare for his call. But the little Harriet had seen of the young men of the town had led her to doubt that anyone under the age of forty would trouble themselves about a mongrel, and so she cheerfully imagined the marquess to be quite old and countrified.

Sarah and Annabelle came home carrying a great many packages and boxes. Harriet did feel they spent far too much money on trifles, but as it was their own money they were spending, she decided to let them have their heads, and perhaps curb them if they had to have another Season before finding husbands.

When Harriet awoke the next morning, she was aware of a change in the sounds coming from outside. There seemed to be a great deal of movement and bustle, and, above it all, the birds were singing on the rooftops.

Harriet leapt from the bed and drew back the curtains. Golden sunlight flooded the room; sunlight gilded the cobbles of the street. She raised the window with some difficulty because the wood had swollen with all the rain and the frame was inclined to stick. Warm, sweet air flowed into the room.

She stretched her arms above her head. It was going to be a beautiful day. Her mind was full of plans. That evening was to see the first of their social engagements, a ball at Lord and Lady Phillips' in Brook Street. Lady Phillips was a fat, friendly lady who had taken a great liking to Harriet.

Harriet, under Rainbird's instructions, had invited her to tea shortly after her arrival in London. Rainbird had said that Lady Phillips was one of the easiest members of the ton to get to know and one of the most pleasant.

Beauty stirred in his basket at the foot of Harriet's bed, and she remembered that the Marquess of Huntingdon was to call.

She took great trouble with her appearance as a courtesy to this elderly gentleman who had been kind enough to show concern for her dog. The twins never rose before two in the afternoon, having adapted to fashionable London hours even before their first social engagement.

Harriet put on one of her new gowns. It was of pale-blue India muslin and tied under her bust with two blue silk ribbons. She twisted her thick, fluffy hair into a knot on top of her head, but mischievous little tendrils escaped and formed a sort of sunny halo about her face.

She was sitting in the front parlour at eleven in the morning, with Beauty at her feet, when Rainbird announced that not only the Marquess of Huntingdon but Lord Vere as well had called to see her.

Two gentlemen entered the room and stood on the threshold. Harriet's blue eyes had all the clear candour of a child's as she looked at them. Her first thought was that both men were very presentable, and she regretted not having roused the twins so that they might be introduced.

In their turn, the marquess and Lord Vere studied Harriet Metcalf. Their first sight of her was one that they were both to remember always. She was sitting in a chintz-covered armchair with Beauty at her feet. The sun, shining through the open window behind her, lit up the aureole of her golden hair. She looked dainty, fresh, and very feminine.

The marquess was, Harriet estimated, in his thirties. He had thick, curling chestnut hair, hazel eyes, a high-bridged nose, and a humorous mouth. His waist was slim, and his legs had been called "the finest in England"—after all, no one ever mentioned a lady's legs in an age when it was not polite to admit such female appendages existed. He was dressed in a blue morning-coat with gold-plated buttons, buff breeches, and hessian boots. His biscuit-coloured waistcoat was buttoned high up under the snowy folds of his intricately tied cravat.

Making a magnificent leg, the marquess said, "We called to see Miss Metcalf."

"I am Miss Metcalf."

Lord Vere looked around the room as if searching for a chaperone. He was slightly shorter than the marquess and had black hair and black eyes. He affected the Byronic style of dress, a fashion described sometimes unkindly as highly expensive sloppiness.

"Are your parents at home, Miss Metcalf?" he asked.

Harriet's blue eyes clouded. "They are both dead," she said. Then her eyes cleared. "Oh, of course you do not know why I am in London. I am godmother to two very beautiful ladies, the Misses Hayner, who are to make their debut at the Season."

"You look much too young to have goddaughters old enough to make their come-out," said the marquess.

"The late Sir Benjamin Hayner," said Harriet, "made me the girls' godmother. I am some years older than they and should really be wearing caps."

Beauty stirred and rolled a bloodshot eye in the direction of the marquess.

"So this is my patient," said the marquess. He fished in his coat pocket and brought out a small phial and a wad of cotton wool and then bent over Beauty.

"Do be careful," said Harriet. "He is inclined to be a little bit bad-tempered with strangers."

But Beauty barely stirred as the marquess gently washed out first one ear and then the other with the solution.

"Now, Miss Metcalf," said the marquess, throwing the soiled cotton wool on the fire and handing Harriet the phial, "treat his ears twice a day for a week, and he will soon be well again."

"You are both very kind," said Harriet, and the marquess looked down into those beautiful blue eyes and felt a twinge of pique that Lord Vere should be included in Miss Metcalf's thanks.

"Pray be seated," added Harriet, ringing the bell. Rainbird, who had been waiting in the hall, answered its summons. Harriet ordered wine and cakes.

The marquess sat down opposite her, but Lord Vere startled Harriet by sitting down on the carpet and, leaning back gracefully, propped himself up on one elbow with one white hand resting negligently on his knee. Harriet had not yet come across the London craze for "lounging."

"We have not seen you at the opera or at any of the functions we have attended this month, Miss Metcalf," said Lord Vere.

"I and the Misses Hayner shall be attending the Phillips' ball this evening," said Harriet with simple pride, for she was pleased that her efforts had produced such a pleasant invitation for herself and the girls.

Both gentlemen remembered that they had refused the invitation to the ball, deciding to play cards at White's instead.

"Shall I see you there?" asked Harriet, nodding to Rainbird to pour the gentlemen glasses of wine.

"Yes, definitely," said the marquess blandly, avoiding a startled look from Lord Vere.

"Sarah and Annabelle Hayner are both charming young ladies," said Harriet. "They are twins."

"Indeed," said Lord Vere with a marked lack of interest.

"You had better sit up, Gilbert," said the marquess with some amusement. "You will slop wine on the carpet if you continue to try to lounge with wine in the one hand and cake in the other."

Lord Gilbert Vere moved up onto a chair and turned again to Harriet. "Are you not afraid to live here, Miss Metcalf?" he asked eagerly.

"No," replied Harriet, puzzled. "Should I be?"

"Don't you know this house has a curse on it?"

"Mr. Gladstone, the lawyer who found it for us, said nothing about a curse."

"Aha! A terrible fate is about to befall you, my pretty," said Lord Vere with a stage leer.

Harriet turned to the marquess. "Are you both funning?" she pleaded. "What is all this about a curse?"

But it was Lord Vere who gleefully related the sinister happenings that had taken place at Number 67 Clarges Street.

Harriet listened, wide-eyed. When Lord Vere had finished, she said, "But many houses older than this have seen brutal and sinister happenings. I do not believe they ever affect anyone who lives in the building afterwards unless they themselves are brutal and sinister or have extremely bad luck."

"There you are, Gilbert," said the marquess with a sweet smile. "My views exactly."

"And you do not believe such things either, Lord Vere," said Harriet with a laugh.

"Oh, yes he does," said the marquess maliciously. "He is a hardened gambler, and all gamblers look for signs and omens."

Lord Vere sent the marquess a smouldering look. "Would you care to go driving with me on the morrow, Miss Metcalf?" he asked.

"Thank you," replied Harriet with a sunny smile. "We should like it above all things."

Lord Vere eyed Beauty nervously. "Forgive me, ma'am, but is that animal used to carriage rides?"

"I did not mean Beauty, of course," laughed Harriet. "I know you meant your invitation to include my god-daughters."

"No, as a matter of fact I did not," said Lord Vere, tugging miserably at his cravat and aware that his friend's sardonic eye was fastened on him. "I have a phaeton and it really seats only two comfortably and so—"

"And so Miss Metcalf will need to endure my company," said the marquess. "I have a barouche which will hold us all very comfortably."

"I could hire a barouche," said Lord Vere sulkily.

"There is no need to go to such expense," said Harriet. "We shall accept Lord Huntingdon's invitation on this occasion, and perhaps one of the Misses Hayner will go out driving with you on another."

"I have not even met the Misses Hayner," said Lord Vere with some acerbity.

Harriet looked puzzled. The marquess realised with some amusement that she was totally unaware of her own looks and thought the attraction must be her two charges. He thought then with some regret that Harriet's brain must be as soft as her appearance, for how could she possibly imagine that two gentlemen would be competing to take out two misses they had not even seen? In this, he did Harriet an injustice. It had been drilled into Harriet's mind from an early age that one's attractions depended entirely on the amount of money one possessed as a dowry. She thought the marquess and Lord Vere must have learned of the Hayners' wealth and were therefore acting in very much the way she would have expected two fashionable gentlemen to behave.

"Never mind," said the marquess gently. "If the weather holds fine, we should have a tolerable drive." He rose to his feet. "Good day, Miss Metcalf. I look forward to seeing you at the ball this evening."

Harriet rose and curtsied.

"May I hope to have the honour of dancing with you?" asked Lord Vere, flashing an angry look at his friend.

Harriet blushed. "I had not thought of dancing myself," she said. "I shall be sitting with the chaperones."

Lord Vere began to protest hotly that one so fair should be condemned to blush unseen, but the marquess said smoothly, "Miss Metcalf will not find herself neglected, Gilbert. I shall be happy to sit with her."

Harriet curtsied low. Rainbird, who had been standing beyond the open door in the hall, leapt to hold the street door open for the gentlemen.

Both men stood on the step, drawing on their gloves.

"Did you need to cut me out so savagely?" said Lord Vere hotly. "You are a philanderer and womaniser, and I want you to leave this one alone."

"Yes, I did behave badly," agreed the marquess equably. "Pray accept my apology. I was near an ame's ace of falling in love with her. Such tenderness, such dewy beauty. But much too simple-minded for my decadent tastes. I shall take Miss Metcalf and her charges driving tomorrow as I promised and then leave the field to you."

Harriet crossed to the window to watch them walk by. She heaved a little sigh. The marquess was so very handsome. But so very practised. He had made his friend look a fool, and that had diminished him in her eyes. But he did look so very like a hero out of a romance, and it was so lowering to reflect that she must never think of herself, but only concentrate on suitable beaux for the twins.

The marquess turned and smiled and looked full at her. It was just as if he expected her to be watching from the window like a . . . like a moonstruck calf, thought Harriet, turning away. It was important that she quickly become fast friends with some of the other chaperones at the ball. It appeared the handsome marquess was a rake. *Not Suitable,* said her mother's voice in her ear. *Not Suitable At All!*

Chapter
Four

*These sort of boobies think that people come to balls
to do nothing but dance; whereas everyone knows
that the real business of a ball is either to look out
for a wife, to look after a wife, or to look after
somebody else's wife.*

—Surtees

Spring had affected the West End of London with a sort of hectic, anticipatory fever. It was like the first night of the Season, instead of merely the beginnings of the preparation for it.

Before the lamplighters had started on their rounds, one could see candles moving like fireflies from room to room of town houses as misses and their maids searched for that all important ribbon, feather, or fan. The smell of hot hair being wound around hundreds of curling tongs scented the air. Liveried footmen darted along the streets conveying messages from Lord this and Miss that. Lambeth Mews, at the end of Clarges Street, was bustling with activity as grooms cleaned out carriages and polished varnish.

Harriet had hired a carriage for the Season, prudently settling on a closed one. The twins had pouted, longing to display their charms in an open carriage to the public, but

Harriet had been unexpectedly firm. The English weather was treacherous; she did not want to waste the Hayners' money on the extravagance of two carriages, nor did she wish her charges to arrive at their destination soaked to the skin.

But after only a few protests, the twins had gracefully given in, as they had to Harriet's very few other strictures. As Harriet took out her gown for the ball, however, she was plagued by a nagging feeling of unease. She had not drawn any closer to Sarah and Annabelle. They were charming to her and always correct, but sometimes she caught them exchanging sideways glances, and it was borne in on her that she did not know what they really thought of her. Then she gave herself a mental shake. They should have been in mourning. Their father had died only a short time ago. It was only natural they should draw together against the world. Harriet had been somewhat shocked when she had first learned that Sir Benjamin did not expect his daughters to wear the willow for him and that he had left strict instructions that they were not even to appear in half mourning.

Harriet had decided to wear something subdued for her first public appearance, as befitted her role of chaperone. She had had a gown of silver-grey tabinet—a watered poplin, half silk, half wool—made up for her. The fashionable dressmaker had nonetheless made it appear, to Harriet's country eyes, too modish an affair, as it was cut low on the bosom, was high-waisted, and ended in three deep flounces.

She wondered whether to ring for Emily, the lady's maid, to help her with her tapes, but decided she would rather dress herself, since there was something about Emily she did not quite like—an uncomfortable feeling for Harriet, who was not in the way of disliking anyone.

She put the curling tongs on the little spirit stove to heat and wondered about the previous tenants of Number 67. What other young ladies had used this room and had prepared for a ball among the rented furniture? Harriet had taken the bedroom next to the dining room on the first floor. Sarah and Annabelle had the front and back bedrooms on the floor above. Harriet's room was dominated by a great double bed and a large William and Mary wardrobe. Although the curtains at the window and the bed hangings were of red silk and the furniture was highly polished, it had the atmosphere of a rented room. There were no pictures or ornaments or any of the cosy clutter one would find in a home.

She shivered slightly in her scanty chemise and bent to put some more coal on the fire. High fashion had not reached the sedate confines of Upper Marcham, and Harriet had been shocked to discover the scantiness of clothing one was expected to wear in London. The *Times* had only recently commented acidly, "The fashion of false bosoms has at least this utility, that it compels our fashionable fair to wear *something.*" Harriet had absolutely refused to wear drawers, a recent innovation she considered highly indecent. Drawers had always been a purely masculine garment. Harriet had settled for a chemise or scanty petticoat—the old term shift was now considered vulgar—which was the only undergarment that most young ladies wore. The chemise was knee length. The neck opening—very low to accommodate the latest fashions—was square and edged with a gathered muslin frill.

She pulled on a pair of pink silk stockings, slid on her garters, and then turned with a sigh to try to do something with her fluffy hair before putting on her ballgown.

She had picked up the first tress and was winding it around the tongs when the Marquess of Huntingdon's face rose before her eyes. She saw his mocking hazel eyes and humorous mouth; she heard that caressing husky note in his voice and started in alarm as her hair, held overlong in the tongs, began to crackle. Harriet sat down on the little needlepoint stool in front of the toilet table, feeling shaken, feeling haunted.

For that one moment, she had felt his presence so strongly, it was as if he had walked into the room and stood over her.

She pressed her soft lips into a determined line. She had done very well so far in preparing to launch Sarah and Annabelle. Miss Spencer would have been amazed at how well she had handled things. She was not going to be thrown off her stride by the seductive wiles of a rake. And Harriet was sure he *was* a rake. From trusting everybody in the whole wide world, Harriet was gradually becoming wary, like a very young animal lost in a savage jungle. There was something wrong about the marquess, something that threatened her quiet life and security.

She seized the tongs and surprised herself by finally achieving quite the prettiest hairstyle she had ever managed to create. She threaded a long silver-grey ribbon among her soft curls to achieve the Grecian effect which was so popular with the ladies of the ton. Firmly keeping her mind focused on the preparations for the ball, she was soon able to banish even the slightest thought about the Marquess of Huntingdon.

England was going through a brief phase of pseudo-democracy, which is why the Marquess of Huntingdon's evening coat did not allow even a glimpse of shirt cuff to be shown. That thin white line that cut the community in two, separating the gentleman of leisure from the manual worker, was thought to be undemocratic. It was a fashion that had come into being seventeen years before, and gentlemen like the marquess had obviously forgotten the reason for it—for there was a splendid sapphire pin waiting on his dresser to be buried among the snowy folds of his starched cravat. Brummell, that famous dandy, had brought starch into fashion. This innovation earned him a mention in the press. "When he first appeared in this stiffened cravat, the sensation was prodigious; dandies were struck dumb with envy and washerwomen miscarried."

Next to Brummell's, the marquess's cravats were the envy of the ton, and, unlike Beau Brummell, the marquess usually had very little difficulty in pleating the starched material into sculptured folds. But for some reason, the magic had left his fingers. He blamed Harriet Metcalf. He could not get her out of his mind. It must be a sign of increasing age, he thought bitterly as he threw another ruined cravat on the floor. He had a clever, witty, and competent mistress; his fortune allowed him to travel; he had worked hard in America and had long dreamed of the frivolity of the London Season; and he was surely experienced enough not to be taken in by an innocent from the country with fair hair and large blue eyes. Harriet Metcalf, he was sure, was that rarest of creatures—a thoroughly good woman—and surely nothing was more boring than that. But he kept remembering her softness, her femininity, and the swell of her bosom. Even her gentle voice sounded in his ears.

He had made up his mind to ignore her at the ball. He did not even want to go to this curst ball, but he had called on a much gratified Lady Phillips to explain he would be there after all, and he had promised Lord Vere he would accompany him. Now he decided that perhaps the best thing would be to seek her out, talk to her, find her as empty-headed and dull as he was sure she would prove to be on closer acquaintance, and then the carriage ride the next day would surely put an end to these strange springlike yearnings.

By ten in the evening, Harriet was seated demurely against the wall with the other chaperones. She was well-content. As the duenna of two formidable dowries, she was welcomed into their ranks and regaled with all the latest gossip. It was rumoured the king had been put in a strait-jacket again and surely poor Prinny would be made Regent now. After all, had not King George fancied himself a Quaker this age and gone about in Quaker dress? And he had not shaved for a long time and looked like Mr. Kemble in King Lear. What did Miss Metcalf think of the fashion of wearing aprons over petticoats for undress?

Harriet chatted away, oblivious of the attention her dazzlingly fair looks were attracting. Many of the gentlemen would have liked to approach her, but she seemed so absorbed in conversation with such a formidable array of harridans that they did not dare. Next to Harriet was Baroness Villiers, a crusty, tetchy old lady whose frivolous granddaughter was at that moment falling over the feet of a guardsman on the floor and laughing immoderately.

"I wish she would not go on like that," said the baroness crossly. "Your girls behave like angels. I wish my Amelia would copy their manners."

"Amelia appears to please the gentlemen," said Harriet. "She has such gay, unaffected manners." She fell silent as she watched Sarah and Annabelle. Harriet had to admit that both were in looks, although she wished that pastel colours, which did not show either girl to advantage, were not quite so fashionable. Sarah was in blue and Annabelle in pink. Sarah was wearing a fine sapphire necklace, and Annabelle boasted a diamond collar. They flirted with their partners to a nicety, all fluttering eyelashes and waving fans.

What a pair of actresses they are, mused Harriet, and then was appalled at her own thought. *London is making me uncharitable,* she chided herself. She turned to the baroness and to her horror found herself wishing that the lady would shave, for the baroness's grey moustache and incipient beard were disconcerting.

"The Marquess of Huntingdon called on me today," said Harriet. "He had met my footman walking my dog and immediately saw that the poor animal was sick. He gave me some lotion. The marquess called with Lord Vere."

"Humph," said the baroness. "Lord Vere is very well. Fine family, good fortune."

"And Lord Huntingdon?"

"A rake, my dear. Keep well clear of him. Do you see Belinda Romney over there? No, no, the one dancing with that tall, gangly fellow? Well, Mrs. Romney is his mistress, newly set up. He gave her those emeralds to match her eyes."

Harriet looked at Mrs. Romney. She was a voluptuous brunette with creamy skin and roguish eyes. Her gown was hitched up on either side to display a pair of pink stockings, and the material of her gown was so filmy that it was easy to see she had nothing on underneath except the stockings.

"And what does Mr. Romney think of the liaison?" asked Harriet.

"He died two years ago, leaving her nothing but debts, so she has done well for herself to secure Huntingdon, and him so lately come to town. He was always generous to his mistresses, I'll say that for the man."

Harriet felt very depressed. Although she had believed the marquess to be a rake, she had hoped to be proved wrong. After all, he had helped Beauty, and that might have shown evidence of a kind heart. But Harriet now could not bring herself to think of him as kind. Mrs. Romney had been left destitute and obviously needed money badly. The marquess had taken advantage of her situation.

On Harriet's other side was Mrs. Cramp, who had two hopeful daughters at the ball. They frequently came bouncing up to speak to their mama and ask her if she was well and to tell her about their partners. Even the baroness's granddaughter, Amelia, came over between dances to chat to her grandmother. Neither Sarah nor Annabelle approached Harriet. In fact, they never once looked in her direction.

"Here comes Huntingdon and Vere," said Mrs. Cramp suddenly. "Isn't Huntingdon enough to make any female swoon? 'Tis a pity he's a rake."

"Yes," said Harriet a little sadly. For the marquess, as he strolled into the ballroom, looked the hero of any woman's dreams, from his handsome face to his small waist and beautiful legs. He was exquisitely tailored and wore his clothes with an air. His face had a slight tan that owed nothing to walnut juice, and his hands were free of paint, unlike those of some of the gentlemen who white-leaded the backs of their hands and painted their palms a delicate pink with cochineal.

Lord Vere would have set off immediately in Harriet's direction, but, by ill chance, a gentleman buttonholed him and started to tell the irritated lord a long and dreary story about what Brummell had said to Lord Alvanley. Lord Vere gloomily listened with half an ear while watching the marquess make his expert way around the edge of the ballroom to where Harriet was sitting. "He told me he wanted nothing to do with her," grumbled Lord Vere.

"Who? What?" demanded the boring gentleman, pausing in the middle of his story.

"What does Huntingdon want?" demanded Mrs. Cramp. Harriet looked up in time to see the marquess bearing down on her.

She looked down again quickly and studied the painted picture on her fan. Then she studied the toes of the marquess's shoes with interest as he came to stand in front of her.

"You do not dance, Miss Metcalf?" he asked.

Harriet raised her blue eyes. "No, my lord, my duty here is as chaperone."

Baroness Villiers and Mrs. Cramp exchanged looks across the top of Harriet's head. They both thought this new member of their ranks a vastly fetching little thing. Huntingdon was a rake with the morals of a tomcat, but it did seem a shame that little Miss Metcalf should have no fun at all. She was surely as young as the debutantes.

"Get along with you," said the baroness heartily. "Your charges are doing very nicely. A lady of your tender years does not belong here with us."

"Do accept Lord Huntingdon's offer," urged Mrs. Cramp, who despite her earlier warning dearly loved a rake. "I shall keep an eye on your goddaughters."

"Very well," said Harriet in a low voice. It seemed easier to go with the marquess than enter into an argument with her new-found friends.

It was a country dance and went on for quite half an hour, which was more than enough time to allow society to see how very well pretty little Miss Metcalf danced, and how much Huntingdon appeared to be enjoying her company.

By chance, both Sarah and Annabelle found themselves partnerless for this dance. They retreated to a corner and unfurled their fans so that they could whisper behind them.

"Well!" exclaimed Sarah angrily. "Who is that divine creature with dreary Harriet?"

"I asked my last partner the minute I saw him enter the ballroom," said Annabelle. "That, beloved Sis, is the Marquess of Huntingdon, vastly rich. A rake."

"Our dear godmother has no right to be dancing about," said Sarah. "It is our come-out, not hers. That dress is quite unsuitable."

Both girls lowered their fans and glared at the tabinet gown of silver grey. It was admittedly very plain, with little embellishment apart from the three deep flounces and a little string of coral beads that Harriet wore about her neck. The neckline was low, but not as low as some of the other gowns being sported. But the elegance of the line showed her figure to advantage, as did the grace of her movements, although neither girl would admit to noticing that latter asset.

Annabelle yawned. As usual, she felt sleepy. "Then perhaps it is time to prime Emily," she said lazily. "Emily is such a good gossip. She passed on everything we had told her about Harriet to the people in the village."

Both girls savoured the memory. "Do you remember," said Sarah, "the haberdasher, Mr. James, who used to turn pink every time he saw Harriet? One would never have thought he would have believed a word against her. But he believed it when Emily told him how Harriet had deliberately courted our father's affections. Emily must have been very convincing."

"I am surprised he believed her," said Annabelle.

"Oh, she did not tell him direct. She burst into tears in the shop and confided in that old harridan, Mrs. Winter, the colonel's lady, and Mr. James asked what the matter was. He didn't believe it at first, but then he got it from one other source before the day was out and then another the next day."

"Well, I don't like the way Harriet is making so free with our money for *her* wardrobe," said Annabelle sourly. "She is wearing an expensive gown and dancing with the handsomest man in the room as if she were the debutante and we the chaperones. I am so hungry. We go in to supper after this dance. So shaming not to have a partner."

"Yes," agreed Sarah absentmindedly, her eyes on Harriet. "I think dear Harriet is getting a little too much attention. Emily is very loyal to us. It would do no harm if she were to start to drop a word here and there, as she did in the village. She can start off in the servants' quarters. And speaking of servants, have you ever seen such an odd crowd? No wonder murder and mayhem have been done at Number Sixty-seven! I saw the cook emerging from the nether regions t'other day, and he looked as if he might slit anyone's throat. That Rainbird is more like a mountebank than a butler, and they do not treat us with the right deference. Servants should be frightened of their masters. Oh, look, the dance is over."

Both girls lowered their fans and flirted with their eyes to such advantage that they soon had two cavaliers at their side to take them into supper.

They would have been amazed to know that their godmother was thoroughly miserable at the thought of eating her supper in the company of Lord Huntingdon. Harriet had been glad that the steps of the energetic country dance had made conversation impossible. Now it appeared she was expected to take supper with the marquess simply because he had partnered her in the dance preceding it. It was not as if he were a suitable *parti* for either of the girls. She would never feel easy in her mind if she thought she had been instrumental in wedding either Sarah or Annabelle to such a hardened rake.

The marquess studied her downcast face and felt himself becoming very angry indeed. He had never quite put himself out so much over any female before and, instead of looking gratified, Miss Metcalf looked as if he were leading her to the gallows rather than into the supper room at a tonnish London ball. His mistress was looking daggers at him, and he knew a stormy scene lay ahead. He wished he had not taken her out of the care of old Lord Brothers. Belinda was delightful, but she was becoming increasingly jealous.

The supper room was decorated in an Indian theme, draped with yards of silk and set about with palm trees.

Voices rose and fell. Harriet looked down at a selection of delicacies on her plate and felt she did not want to eat any of it. She was aware of the marquess's eyes on her face. She was aware too of the strength of his personality, a personality which seemed to be seeking to dominate her. Harriet had been used to being ordered around. Her parents had laid down the law on every subject, and, after their death, Sir Benjamin had fallen into the way of ordering her about. Even Josephine—Miss Spencer—had, on occasion, affectionately called Harriet a widgeon and had stepped in to tackle her problems for her. But since she had come to London, her desire to do the best for Sarah and Annabelle had given Harriet a new courage and independence. Unknown to herself, she was on the brink of discovering she preferred to make up her own mind.

"Where is your home, Miss Metcalf?" she realised the marquess was asking.

"Upper Marcham, a small village in Barshire."

"And do you see much social life there?"

"Not since my parents died, which was some seven years ago," said Harriet. "Before that, they took me to assemblies in Barminster."

"I am amazed you are still unwed."

The candid blue eyes that looked up into his own had an expression of wonder in them, as if still astonished by the whole wide world. "Why, sir," she said, "I have no dowry."

"I would have thought your face was dowry enough," he said. His voice was warm and teasing; the voice, thought Harriet, of a practised flirt.

"No one's face is enough, my lord," she said sharply.

"Come, I cannot believe no one has ever proposed to you."

"Yes, they did, when my parents were alive, but Mama considered them unsuitable."

"And what did you think?"

Harriet looked at him in surprise. "I did n-not think anything," she faltered. "One must always honour one's parents' judgement."

"Even if the heart is engaged?"

"I do not think hearts have much to do with marriage," said Harriet. "A lady must marry someone suitable. If her heart is also engaged, then she may count herself fortunate."

49

"But you do not seem to think many such fortunate ladies exist?"

"No, love seems to be something found outside marriage—as in your own case."

She turned brick red.

"Some wine, Miss Metcalf?" he said smoothly while inwardly fuming. But, then, he had only himself to blame. This is what came of encouraging rustic beauties to be impertinent. But it was so very hard to remain angry with her when she looked so ashamed and downcast. Her rare combination of innocence and sensuality was beginning to stir his senses. But it would not answer. He did not wish to be married. He had been married once, such a long time ago, to pretty Dorothy, a tiny charmer, who had died of consumption and saved him the pain of divorcing her for her blatant faithlessness. And Dorothy had once been as innocent as this Miss Metcalf. Women were all the same; once the bloom was lost, they turned into heartless sluts. And Miss Metcalf, for all her innocence, showed a decidedly mercenary turn of mind.

"I apologise for my last remark," said Harriet stiffly. "It—it—just came out."

"Your apology is accepted," he said. "Perhaps you will find a husband this Season, Miss Metcalf."

"I am only interested in finding husbands for the Misses Hayner," said Harriet, "although I do not expect any difficulty. Both are so charming and talented."

"And where are these paragons?"

Harriet nodded her head in the direction of the right-hand corner of the room. "Sarah is the one in blue, and Annabelle is in pink. They are twins."

Her voice glowed with pride. The marquess put down the quizzing glass he had raised to study the girls. He thought they looked like every other insipid debutante he had ever met. He found himself hoping they were worthy of the love and pride with which Miss Harriet Metcalf viewed them.

"You are not eating," he said, looking at her untouched plate.

"I have lost my appetite."

The marquess smiled into her eyes. "May I hope that I have taken your appetite away?"

"No, you may not," said Harriet roundly. "And what a silly thing to hope for anyway."

Both stared at each other in amazement—Harriet just as surprised at her rudeness as the marquess evidently was.

"Don't apologise again," said the marquess. "Let us talk about something perfectly safe, like the weather."

"Or we can talk to Lord Vere instead of each other," said Harriet.

"Or we could if he were here."

"Which he is," said a voice behind the marquess. Lord Vere had come up on them and showed every evidence of joining them.

"I thought you were entertaining Miss Johnson," said the marquess, making room for his friend.

"I was, but I clumsily knocked wine down her gown, and so poor Miss Johnson has gone to repair the damage."

The marquess gave Lord Vere a thoughtful look, as if wondering whether his friend had tipped wine down his partner's gown in order to extricate himself.

"How is your dog?" asked Lord Vere.

"He seems a little recovered," said Harriet. "I feel so ashamed, you know, not having noticed he was unwell. Rainbird, our butler, said he often took away poor Beauty's bowl of food back to the kitchens himself and noticed it had barely been touched. I asked him why he did not inform me of this earlier, and he said he thought the animal had a poor appetite and normally ate very little."

"It is understandable that you should be preoccupied with the serious matter of bringing two young ladies out," said Lord Vere, his black eyes alight with admiration. "They are a credit to you, Miss Metcalf. They were pointed out to me, and I was impressed by their pretty manners."

51

"How good of you to say so!" said Harriet. She picked up her fork and absentmindedly began to eat a little food. "I confess I have been very worried as to how to go on. I do not have any knowledge of the great world, but people have proved remarkably kind."

"I think you bring out the best in all of us," said Lord Vere, and Harriet accepted the compliment with a charming, rippling laugh.

The marquess had never been cut out by any gentleman before, but he had to admit that Gilbert, Lord Vere, had the best of him on this occasion. The two subjects closest to Harriet's heart seemed to be her mangy dog and her giggling goddaughters.

Lord Vere had placed himself between the marquess and Harriet. He turned towards her in such a way as almost to block her from the marquess's view.

"I am sorry I shall not have the pleasure of driving out with you tomorrow," he said. "But may I call on you?"

"Of course," said Harriet with a smile. "Sarah and Annabelle will be delighted to make your acquaintance."

"Do you plan to go to the opera?" asked Lord Vere.

"I must rent a box. I have not yet done so and . . . and I believe the patrons of the opera are very high sticklers, quite like Almack's, and as I was not very sure how to go about it, I rather put things off."

"Miss Metcalf, I would be proud to arrange the rental of a box for you. There will be no trouble with the patrons. London has not seen such beauty for many a Season."

"How charming of you to say so," said Harriet, her eyes glowing. "I shall convey your compliment to Sarah and Annabelle."

The marquess looked cynically amused. It was obvious to him that Gilbert was longing to tell the naïve Miss Metcalf that he had meant the compliment for her but now decided it would be churlish to do so. The marquess also felt a stab of annoyance that she should appear so relaxed and at ease in Gilbert's company. But Harriet's only interest in Lord Vere was as a prospective beau for either Sarah or Annabelle. She liked his easy and unaffected manners. He was handsome, but not in the disturbing and compelling way that the marquess was handsome. She felt happy in his company and wished the marquess would go away.

As if sensing her thoughts, the marquess rose, bowed, and took his leave. As he walked in the direction of the card room, he told himself firmly that Harriet Metcalf had proved to be as boring and naïve as he had expected. She was not worth another thought.

But neither, it appeared, was any other woman at the ball. The handsome marquess settled down with his friends for a rubber of whist, forgetting even his mistress, Belinda Romney—Belinda, who watched Harriet with jealous eyes and blamed this newcomer to the London scene for the coldness and indifference of her usually attentive lover.

Chapter Five

And when I feigned an angry look,
Alas! I loved you best.

—John Sheffield
Duke of Buckingham and Normandy

What screams, what pinches, what giggles, what oh-you-naughty-pusses were inflicted on Harriet by Sarah and Annabelle after the ball when she told them the story of Beauty's rescuer. Never had the twins been more in charity with their godmother. Never had their vanity been so rampant. To them it was all too plain. Both gentlemen had cultivated the acquaintance of Harriet in order to secure introductions to themselves. For who could possibly believe that the devastatingly handsome and devastatingly rich Marquess of Huntingdon would be in the slightest interested in the welfare of a cur like Beauty?

And Harriet had behaved just as she ought, that much they admitted as they prepared for bed. There would be a stay of execution. No need to ruin Harriet's reputation while Harriet continued to perform so admirably. Before leaving the ball, Lord Vere had told Harriet he would call at three in the afternoon; the marquess was to call at a quarter to five.

Both girls argued over the merits of these beaux and then amicably decided that Sarah should have Lord Huntingdon and Annabelle, Lord Vere.

They could hardly sleep for excitement. Dresses were planned. Then there were portfolios of watercolours to be arranged and needlework to be displayed.

The servants discussed the forthcoming visits over breakfast in the servants' hall the next morning. They gossiped and talked with much of their usual freedom, for Emily, the lady's maid, was not present, and although only Lizzie, the scullery maid, actively disliked her, the others were only conscious of a lifting of a certain restraint which her presence imposed on the "family."

"It would be a great feather in Miss Metcalf's cap if she could secure just one of them for either Miss Sarah or Miss Annabelle," said Rainbird.

"Perhaps their interest lies in Miss Metcalf," suggested Mrs. Middleton. "She is quite beautiful and so sweet and courteous."

"Perhaps it would be best not to say such a thing when Emily is present," volunteered Lizzie shyly. "I do not think she likes Miss Metcalf."

"And what do you know of the grend world, you with your scrubbing brush?" jeered Joseph. MacGregor, the cook, saw Lizzie wince and slammed a cup of tea down in front of the footman with unnecessary force.

"What do you mean, Lizzie?" asked Rainbird, casting a threatening look at the footman.

"Only that there is a certain something about Emily," said Lizzie cautiously. "Alice was saying the other day that Miss Metcalf was the nicest, sweetest lady any servant had ever waited on, and Emily said nothing, but I saw her lip curl."

"That's because you don't work hard enough," said Mrs. Middleton. "You have too much time on your hands, young Lizzie, and you indulge in fancies about your betters." A lady's maid, in the servants' strict hierarchy, *was* a scullery maid's better. Mrs. Middleton privately thought Lizzie a very good worker indeed, but she nourished hopes of elevating the girl should their circumstances change and was apt to cover her very real affection for Lizzie with a brusque and authoritarian manner.

"Perhaps you are right," said Lizzie listlessly, and Rainbird looked at her sharply. The scullery maid's hair had lost its sheen, and her face was so pale it was almost greenish in the gloom of the servants' hall.

"What our Lizzie needs is some fresh air," said Rainbird. "Go and take a walk in the Park, Lizzie. Dave will help out with your duties."

"Can she take thet dog with her?" asked Joseph eagerly. "It don't do my position no good being seen with a mangy cur like thet. Luke is always teasing me." Luke, Joseph's friend and rival, worked next door as Lord Charteris's first footman.

"I don't mind," said Lizzie quickly, seeing Rainbird was about to protest. Lizzie would have done anything to please the feckless and vain Joseph.

"Well, don't let the beast near the kitchen," said Joseph ungratefully. "Meh cat must not be tormented."

"Why don't you marry the flea bag?" said the cook sourly. "The Moocher is the only thing you care about apart from your worthless self. Jessamy."

Joseph scowled at the insult. Jessamy, a corruption of jessamine or jasmine, was applied to the weak and effeminate. The Moocher rubbed himself against the cook's legs, and Angus MacGregor absentmindedly bent down and stroked the animal. He, too, was fond of the kitchen cat because the Moocher was a mouser supreme.

It was unthinkable that Lizzie should show her undistinguished presence abovestairs, so Rainbird went to fetch Beauty and told Lizzie to meet him at the top of the area steps.

Somewhere down in the depths of Joseph's self-cen-

tred soul twitched the faint stirrings of a bad conscience.
"It's very good of you, Lizzie," he said awkwardly. "The
brute is as quiet as a lamb. You won't have any trouble."

"Here, give the dog this bone when you've got him in
Green Park," said MacGregor. "They aye take to someone
who feeds 'em."

He wrapped a marrow bone up in an old page of the
Times and handed it to Lizzie.

"And put your shawl on," said Mrs. Middleton sharply,
for she too had just noticed how sickly the scullery maid
looked.

When Lizzie emerged from the basement some ten
minutes later it was to find Rainbird already waiting with
Beauty on a leash. Rainbird thoughtfully watched girl and
dog walk down Clarges Street in the direction of the Green
Park. He realised that all winter long he had been too
wrapped up in fantasies about Felice to notice much that
was going on about him. Felice, the French lady's maid who
had graced Number 67 the year before, had won her dowry
and independence from service and had settled in Brighton. She had refused Rainbird's offer of marriage, but she
was still unwed, and Rainbird hoped she might change her
mind. Now the Season was here, and there was no chance
of a day off to go to Brighton until it was all over.

He decided, if Lizzie should still look ailing in a few
days' time, to take her over to an apothecary's in the City.
Servants went to doctors only in extreme emergencies, as
one visit to even the most undistinguished physician might
take away a whole year's wages.

The day was sunny and warm but still had that slight
tinge of cold somewhere in the soft wind to remind Lon-
doners that, although it looked as if spring had arrived, a
return to winter could be right behind it.

Lizzie found she was beginning to feel better already.
She took her shawl down from her head and wrapped it
about her shoulders, enjoying the warm feel of the sun on

her hair. Beauty was such a placid, amiable sort of dog, and it was pleasant to have company.

She decided, instead of crossing Piccadilly to the Green Park, to take Beauty to Hyde Park, where she could enjoy watching the aristocracy riding in the Row.

Beauty, plodding beside her, felt the warm sun on his coat. He cautiously shook his head. There was no pain at all. He gave it a tremendous shake. Not only was he free of that sharp, stabbing pain, but he could once again hear perfectly. His stomach gave a healthy canine rumble. He was hungry and this human beside him smelled deliciously of marrow bone. Slowly, his ridiculous plume of a tail curled up over his back. Up came his head, and his wicked little bearlike eyes roamed about, looking for trouble.

Unaware of the metamorphosis that was going on somewhere down about knee-level, Lizzie continued on in the direction of the park, enjoying the soft luxurious sensation given by a pair of new leather shoes. When Rainbird had received the glad tidings of the servants' increase in wages, he had not been so far lost in fantasies about Felice to neglect to reward the staff. Alice and Jenny were given silk ribbons; Mrs. Middleton, a new cap. Dave got a new leather waistcoat; Joseph, a silk handkerchief; and Angus MacGregor, a new Sheffield-steel carving knife. And Lizzie, who had worn nothing but clogs before, was given a pair of shiny black-leather shoes with cheap tin buckles.

Lizzie was very religious, and the Lord her God was a terrible God, always just up there on the clouds waiting to blast the vain sinner. Later on, when she thought of the terrible events of that morning, Lizzie was sure He had punished her for her False Pride.

She crossed Park Lane and made her way into Hyde Park. The trees were covered in a delicate haze of green, and the scent from the blossom on the cherry trees made her head swim deliciously. She bent down and slipped Beauty's leash, unwrapped the marrow bone and gave it to him, spread her shawl on the grass near the Row, and sat down. MacGregor had given Lizzie the wrong bone. The one he had given her had been set aside to make stock and still had a large piece of meat attached to it. Beauty gnawed and tore at it, feeling the warmth of the meat descending to his thin belly, feeling the sun on his coat, occasionally shaking his head to make sure the dreadful pain had gone.

He licked the last piece of marrow from the bone and then rolled over and laid his head on Lizzie's lap and gazed up at her with eyes moist with love. For surely this goddess was responsible for his well-being. Lizzie carelessly stroked his narrow head, thinking what a mean, ill-favoured beast he was and wondering how anyone as beautiful and dainty as Miss Metcalf could own such a pet. Miss Metcalf, mused Lizzie, who had only seen her once, was so pretty and sweet that she reminded you of all the good safe things in life, like spring flowers and new bread, honey from the comb and strong tea—those being the things the little scullery maid held most dear next to Joseph.

The Row had been empty, as few of the fashionables stirred from their bed before noon.

Then Lizzie heard the thud of horses' hooves and looked up. Two people, a man and a woman, came galloping down the Row. Lizzie had a quick impression of a tall handsome man and a pretty woman in a scarlet riding habit before disaster struck. Beauty's ruff went up, and he was off like a shot, snapping and snarling at the heels of the lady's horse, which reared in fright and tossed her from its back. The gentleman reined in his own mount and leapt down. Lizzie rushed forward and grabbed the snarling and growling Beauty, leashed him, tied him to a sapling, and then miserably ran forward to where the gentleman was kneeling beside the lady.

A pair of furious hazel eyes glared into her own and a voice like ice said, "Cannot you control your dog?" He turned to the lady and said, "Are you hurt, Belinda?"

The lady called Belinda said waspishly, "No, I am not, and no thanks to this vulgar creature here. Call the watch, Huntingdon, and have her dragged off to the round-house."

Lizzie's eyes dilated with fright, and she tried to choke out an apology, and then to the marquess's fury, she fainted dead away.

"You are a fool, Belinda," he said. "Let me help you up. The matter is not so great that you must frighten little servant girls with threats of prison."

Belinda Romney sprang to her feet and brushed the dirt from her riding dress. "This is too much," she raged. "First you cut me at the Phillips' ball while you make a fool of yourself over that Metcalf female, and now, when I am nigh killed, you call me a fool. Well, that dog is going to receive the whipping he deserves."

She advanced on Beauty, her riding crop raised. But the marquess recognised Harriet's dog. He agreed with Belinda that the animal needed a whipping, but for some reason he could not bear to see his mistress strike Harriet Metcalf's pet. He caught her arm and swung her round. "No, Belinda," he said. "No scenes. The one I had to endure last night was enough."

Lizzie stirred at his feet and moaned faintly. He knelt down beside her and lifted her head from the grass.

He was aware of Belinda's stormy departure, aware she had every right to be furious with him.

Lizzie recovered consciousness. "I am so sorry," she whispered. "The dog . . . he had been so quiet. I had no idea he would be so bad."

"Fortunately for you," said the marquess grimly, "I know that animal and know he has been sick since he arrived in London. Come and I will set you on your road."

He helped Lizzie to her feet, but she swayed again and would have fallen if he had not had a firm grip on her.

He gave an exclamation of annoyance and shouted for

his groom, who usually stayed a discreet distance away when he was out riding with Belinda. "Fetch my carriage," he called. "This servant is unwell."

"Look, child," he said, giving Lizzie a little shake, "no one is going to send you to prison. Instead, you will be safely conveyed back to Sixty-seven Clarges Street—that is where you work, is it not?"

"Yes, sir," whispered Lizzie. "Scullery maid."

The Marquess of Huntingdon did not expect Harriet to be awake, for it was only ten in the morning when he returned to Clarges Street with Lizzie and Beauty—London's equestriennes such as Mrs. Romney being the only ones who rose so early. But when he carried Lizzie into the hall, Harriet came running down the stairs in her undress, her hair loose about her shoulders. He found himself staring and said sharply, "Your dog, ma'am, nearly caused a bad accident."

"The girl!" gasped Harriet. "That is one of my servants." She had been introduced to all the staff by Rainbird on her arrival and remembered the little scullery maid who had stood so shyly at the end of the reception line.

"The girl has not been hurt, but she fainted."

Rainbird came hurriedly forward. "Allow me, my lord," he said, lifting Lizzie's slight body from the marquess's arms. "I shall take her belowstairs."

"Very well," said Harriet. "Bring refreshments to the drawing room." She had learned to grace the front parlour by that grander name. "Tell Mrs. Middleton I shall come to see the girl as soon as possible. What is her name?"

"Lizzie."

"If you think Lizzie requires the services of a physician, then by all means summon one. My lord, do not stand in this cold hall." She led the way into the parlour.

Harriet was wearing a nightgown with one of the fashionable aprons which had come into vogue for undress. The nightgown was made high at the neck and had long sleeves. Harriet had found one was expected to wear more in bed than out of it. She raised her arms and hurriedly screwed her hair up into a knot on top of her head.

"Pray be seated," she said to the marquess, "and tell me what happened."

"I was riding in the Row with a certain Miss Romney . . ." He broke off and raised his thin eyebrows, studying the pink rising in Harriet's cheeks and noticing the sudden compression of her soft mouth. So little Miss Metcalf had already found out about his mistress. "Your dog attacked her mount, and she was thrown."

"Was she badly hurt?" asked Harriet.

"Mrs. Romney was fortunate, Miss Metcalf. Only in her pride."

"And Lizzie?"

"My companion was naturally in a rage. She threatened to have your maid dragged off to a roundhouse."

"Poor Lizzie. She is little more than a child."

"A sick child, I fear. Did you not notice the unnatural pallor of her skin?"

"I did not," said Harriet, feeling dreadful. "I never go to the kitchens. I only saw the girl once on my arrival. Oh, how thoughtless and uncaring I seem. First Beauty and now Lizzie. And Miss Romney? Perhaps I should call on her to offer my apologies."

"I think not, ma'am."

"No, no, of course not," said Harriet miserably. "Miss Romney is your mistress, is she not?"

"Curb your tongue, Miss Metcalf, or have you as little control over it as you have over that pesky dog?"

Beauty oiled up to the marquess, licked his hand, and drew back his black lips in a sycophantic smile.

The marquess scrubbed at the back of his hand with a handkerchief. "That animal looks almost human. Does he always smile like that?"

"I had not noticed. I did not think animals capable of smiling. I think he just looks as if he is."

"Where did you find such an unusual lapdog?"

"It was after my parents died. They had the typhoid, you see. Papa would not clear out the cesspool. He said the gentry should have a mind above such things. Papa was always saying things like that. It made Sir Benjamin laugh, and I remember at the time wishing that Sir Benjamin would press Papa to do some practical things instead of always laughing at him. In any case, Mama and Papa died, and I learned I should have to sell up and move to a small cottage and that I would not be able to afford any servants. I am quite capable of looking after myself, but . . . but I did feel so lonely, and I found Beauty in a sack with a litter of other puppies by the side of the river. Someone had thrown the sack from the bridge with the puppies in it, but it had missed the water. Only Beauty was alive. . . ." Her voice trailed away, and she looked down at her hands.

"You said you were lonely," prompted the marquess, "but surely the Misses Hayner called on you."

"I could not really expect them to call at my little cottage," said Harriet. "But I did see them when Sir Benjamin was at home, for he always invited me to dine at Chorley Hall."

"But there are other people in this village, surely."

"Of course, but very few gentry, practically none, and I am afraid my parents were very high sticklers and would associate only with Sir Benjamin, considering everyone else beneath them. But there is a Miss Spencer, who is a very dear friend of mine. I became acquainted with her after I had taken Beauty as a pet, so I am now not lonely at all. And here in London I have Sarah and Annabelle. Here is Rainbird. May I offer you a glass of wine, Lord Huntingdon?"

"Thank you." The marquess watched Harriet while Rainbird poured him a glass of canary. He waited until the butler had left and then he said, "May I offer you a word of advice, Miss Metcalf? Unless you learn to curb your unruly tongue, then I fear you will end up with only your dog for company."

"But I have never said such things to anyone before," said Harriet ingenuously. "Only to you."

"What have I done to merit such unbridled honesty?"

Harriet tilted her head a little to one side and studied him thoughtfully.

"I think it is because you irritate me, my lord, and also because you have a great reputation as a rake."

Harriet sat, appalled. What on earth had come over her! Her eyes filled with tears.

He set down his glass carefully on the table and got to his feet. "Miss Metcalf," he said, studying the top of her bent head, "I have promised to take you driving this afternoon and take you driving I will. But after that, I hope and trust you will avoid my company on every occasion. I shall certainly do my best to avoid yours."

Harriet felt a stab of fear. The girls had been so very happy, so very elated at the prospect of meeting the Marquess of Huntingdon. When she had timidly mentioned his reputation, they had both laughed her to scorn. The only gentlemen worth having were rakes, Sarah had said with that worldly-wise air of hers that always made Harriet feel like a country bumpkin.

She rose and sank into a curtsy. Her blue eyes swimming with tears were raised to his own. "Please accept my deepest, my most humble apology," said Harriet.

He took a step towards her. He wanted to take her in his arms and crush her against him, to feel that soft body against the length of his own. And then he backed away, feeling like some awful slavering satyr. Without a word, he turned on his heel and walked out.

Harriet sat down in the chair again and indulged in a hearty burst of tears. She was a failure. She had learned enough of the World to know that this dashing marquess was a leader of the ton. If she had slapped Beau Brummell's face in the middle of Almack's, she could not possibly have done more damage to her social reputation.

After a few minutes, Harriet dried her eyes. The damage was done. All she could do was promise to school her tongue and behave as prettily as possible when he called again that afternoon. Sarah and Annabelle must never know how badly she had behaved. They would be so disappointed in her!

Then Harriet remembered Lizzie, the scullery maid, and took herself off down to the servants' hall. Beauty, overcome with his exertions, had fallen asleep and did not try to follow her.

There was only Mrs. Middleton and Angus MacGregor in the servants' hall.

"Where is Lizzie?" asked Harriet.

"She is lying down on her bed," said Mrs. Middelton, curtsying. "She will be about her duties soon."

"I do not think she should rise from her bed this day," said Harriet, looking worried. "You may engage more help if you wish. Where is Lizzie's room?"

"She doesn't have a room, ma'am, there being so little space, but she has her pallet in the scullery."

"Please show me where she is," said Harriet.

Mrs. Middleton led the way. Lizzie tried to struggle up when she saw Harriet. Harriet looked sadly down at the thin straw mattress on which Lizzie lay.

"I must ask you to rise for a little, Lizzie," she said gently. "Perhaps, Mrs. Middleton, you could help me lift her."

"Bring a chair, Angus," called Mrs. Middleton. Once Lizzie was lifted onto the chair, Harriet bent down and raised the thin mattress. Straw was sticking out all over it and the underside was damp.

"Are you sure there is nowhere else she could sleep?" asked Harriet, looking worried.

"We don't have the space," said Mrs. Middleton. "She's only a scullery maid, so it is not as if she can move in with me."

"I think," said Harriet, "a truckle bed with fresh blankets is needed here. Please fetch Mr. Rainbird."

But Rainbird entered at that moment with a physician. The staff and Harriet retired to the servants' hall while the doctor examined Lizzie.

At last he came out and said, "The girl has merely caught a bad chill from sleeping on damp straw. Get her something dry to sleep on, and I will give you a resorative cordial for her." Then he cheerfully told Harriet he would send her his bill and bustled off.

The butler said with Miss Metcalf's permission, he would purchase a truckle bed that very day.

Later, when Lizzie was tucked up in her new bed, the servants discussed her health in low voices. They had not realised how badly off little Lizzie had been, sleeping on that dreadful mattress, but servants had their rigid caste system and after all were more callous to their inferiors than any lord or lady.

But soon they were too busy to worry about Lizzie, running hither and thither, as the house prepared for those two all-important callers. Harriet sent up a prayer that the marquess would not, please not, talk about her rude and bold behaviour all over London. Enough to be snubbed by him, but how ruinous for poor innocent Sarah and Annabelle to be snubbed by everyone else.

By the time Lord Vere called, Harriet was in a miserable state, imagining she had brought down social disaster on the twins' heads. She was subdued and so colourless that Lord Vere, in an effort to raise her spirits, made much of her two darling goddaughters, flirting with them and flattering them. He went so far as to try to pat Beauty, but even that brave gesture failed to raise a smile on Harriet's lovely face. At last, it was time to take his leave. He assured Harriet he would engage a box at the opera for her. He longed to have words with her in private, to find out what had distressed her so much, and resolved to call the next day early in the morning when he could be sure of finding her irritating charges still in bed.

It was too early to go on the strut in Bond Street, too early to drive a carriage in the Park. Lord Vere set out for the Marquess of Huntingdon's town house, which was an undistinguished building in Charles Street, the marquess belonging to the breed of aristocrat who considered money spent on town property a waste of time.

He found the marquess in his library, going through a pile of bills and invitations.

"Why so gloomy?" asked the marquess, glancing up at his friend's lowering face.

"I have just been paying a call on Miss Metcalf."

"Ah, that explains everything," said the marquess, leaning back in his chair and clasping his hands behind his head. "Quite a little shrew is our country blossom."

"How can you say that?" demanded Lord Vere. "She was sweetness itself, but so unhappy, so miserable, I longed to get her alone so that I might beg her to tell me what ailed her."

"I'll tell you," said the marquess with a malicious grin. He outlined the morning's events, ending up with a description of Harriet's rude remarks.

"You must have goaded her quite dreadfully," said Lord Vere. "And she was so wretched."

"Of course she was," said the marquess cynically. "She must fear my broadcasting her social gaucherie to the ton, and that would most certainly be social damnation for those two dreary debutantes of hers."

"But you would not!" cried Lord Vere. "Miss Metcalf is unaccustomed to our ways. In the country, it is not the practise to flaunt one's mistress openly in public."

"When were you last in the country, dear boy?" said the marquess. "The woods and copses of England are thick with members of the Fashionable Impure. One cannot enjoy a peaceful dinner with the Quorn without some jade rapping on the dining room window and crying her favours."

"But she is so innocent, so easily hurt . . ."

"Then she should learn not to hurt others. It is only human to want to retaliate."

"But you will not!"

"No, not I. After this afternoon, I shall cut Miss Metcalf dead."

Chapter Six

About three o'clock or four o'clock the fashionable world gives some sign of life, issuing forth to pay visits, or rather leave cards at the doors of friends, never seen but in the crowd of assemblies; to go to the shops, see sights, or lounge in Bond Street—an ugly inconvenient street, the attractions of which it is difficult to understand.

—Louis Simmond

Harriet was in a terrible state of nerves as the time approached for the arrival of the Marquess of Huntingdon. She was now sure he would not come.

Sarah and Annabelle sat attired in thin muslins and ribbons and modish bonnets.

"Tell me, Sarah," essayed Harriet timidly, "would you be so very disappointed if Lord Huntingdon did not come?"

"Stoopid. He *is* coming, so what's to do?"

Harriet glanced nervously at the clock. It lacked one minute to the quarter to five. She took a deep breath. "A most unfortunate thing happened today—"

"There he is!" cried Sarah, rushing to the window.

Harriet stood up, drawing on her gloves. "We should go and join him," she said. "Gentlemen do not like to keep their horses standing."

The marquess, however, had his coachman up on the box, having decided to do the thing properly. Harriet, as befitted her role as duenna, sat with her back to the horses while Sarah, Annabelle, and the marquess sat facing her.

He felt he should cross over and join Miss Metcalf, but he was sure it would start all sorts of female chatter and protests. Sarah and Annabelle realised only too late that they had put themselves at a certain disadvantage by taking the best seats. Although they were on either side of the marquess, both were wearing the very latest thing in poke bonnets, which acted like horse blinkers, and each had to twist around quite uncomfortably to catch even a glimpse of Lord Huntingdon's face.

Harriet, who was wearing a charming little straw confection with a wisp of a veil that fluttered against her face, had a full and uninterrupted view of the marquess.

"The weather is very fine, is it not?" said Harriet.

"Yes, indeed," he said equably. "I trust there will be no further storms or squalls."

"I can assure you, my lord," said Harriet, not meeting his eyes, "that you may have no fear of a recurrence of bad weather."

"Good," he said with a sudden blinding smile.

Sarah fidgeted angrily. What a bore Harriet was! Prosing on about the weather.

"Did you see Mrs. Siddons in *The Country Girl?*" she asked the marquess.

He began to tell them his views on the play and Mrs. Siddons's performance. Sarah and Annabelle hung on his every word. Harriet heaved a little sigh of relief and turned her attention to her surroundings, feeling free to enjoy the view. She was very lucky to have such well-bred charges. The marquess need have no fear that either of them would utter any impolite remarks. And so Harriet gazed happily up at the new leaves as the carriage rolled under the trees in Hyde Park and dreamed of seeing Sarah and Annabelle at a double wedding. She suddenly knew that the marquess had no intention of taking revenge on her by ruining her socially. The pale sunlight shone down on the glittering carriages and glittering jewels of their occupants. There were so many things to see, and it was lovely to sit in a well-sprung carriage and feel the warmth of the spring air and smell the blossoms after such a long and dreary winter.

Harriet's thoughts swung back to the marquess. It was a pity he was so unsuitable, but if he proposed to one of the girls, then she would need to give her permission. Sarah did not mind the idea of a rake for a husband and would probably behave like most society wives after marriage and turn a blind eye to her husband's indiscretions.

But that would not do for me, thought Harriet with a smile. She looked across at the marquess and started as she met the angry glare of his eyes.

The marquess was furious with Harriet. He felt he was behaving very prettily towards her charges, but what right had Miss Metcalf not only to completely ignore him, but to sit there with that silly smile on her stupid face, exactly as if she were dreaming of someone else?

Her eyes dropped before his, and she sat there, subdued, pliant, the very picture of submissive and sensual womanhood. Despite himself, he felt his senses quicken. He looked at Harriet and wondered what she would look like naked. His own thoughts shocked him. The trouble was, he decided, that Harriet Metcalf, with her sweet, innocent air, her soft, swaying pliancy, and the troubled vulnerability in those huge blue eyes brought all the most primitive lusts rising in the masculine breast.

Well, Gilbert certainly seemed to have fallen head over heels for her, but in a purely romantic way. Good luck to Gilbert. He, Huntingdon, would not stand in his way. Annabelle had just essayed a pun, and Sarah was joining her in a wild fit of giggles. The marquess smiled and said such beauty combined with wit quite overset him. Sarah slapped him painfully on the wrist with her fan, and she and Annabelle went off into another peal of laughter.

Wretched, boring little creatures, thought the marquess. But were they so very awful? They were behaving exactly as he had come to expect young ladies of the ton to go on. Liveliness and spirit and a certain amount of unconventionality were to be found in the demi-monde. One would not expect one's wife, say, to go around being as openly and brutally honest as Harriet Metcalf.

He could see it now. "Good morning, my love. Did you sleep well?" "No, Huntingdon, you snored prodigiously and gave me the headache." "I must go out to my club, my sweeting. I promised Brummell his revenge at piquet." "You are not going to your club, my lord, you are going to call on a demi-rep whom you have had in keeping this age."

"Have I said something I ought not to?" asked Sarah, peering up from the long poke of her bonnet like a ferret staring out of its hole. "You look so very angry."

"I think my spleen is disordered."

Both Sarah and Annabelle murmured noises of sympathy. Everything out of sorts was put down to disorders of the spleen.

Even Harriet began to show some interest. "My friend, Miss Spencer, suffers badly from such a disorder," she said. "She went to Bath to take the waters, and she said they were most efficacious."

"Thank you," said the marquess dryly. "If my problem becomes worse I shall repair to Bath."

Harriet lowered her eyes again before the rather predatory gleam in his, not realising they had had their first marital quarrel in the marquess's imagination.

Carriages began to stop beside theirs. First Lord and Lady Phillips, then the Baroness Villiers, then Mrs. Cramp with her daughters, and then none other than the Countess Lieven, one of the most formidable patronesses of Almack's. Harriet braced herself to be on her best and most modest behaviour, when the marquess performed the introductions, and was delighted to notice that Annabelle and Sarah seemed to please the grande dame mightily, perhaps because, although Harriet would not quite admit this to herself, the Countess Lieven obviously liked toad-eaters.

Feeling that vouchers to the all-important Almack's assembly rooms were now secure, Harriet felt quite dizzy with success and gave the marquess such a glowing smile that he smiled back and began to forget that he had ever vowed to cut her dead.

But by the time he returned them to Clarges Street, he felt he was regaining some of his sanity. It would be cruel to try to cut Gilbert out with the pretty chaperone unless his own affections were seriously engaged. Once well away from Harriet, he felt free of her spell. The best thing he could do for Gilbert, Lord Vere, was to leave the field open to him.

But the Marquess of Huntingdon was to become embroiled in Miss Metcalf's affairs sooner than he thought.

Joseph, while they had all been in Hyde Park, had been taking Beauty for a walk in the Green Park. He had not wanted to take the dog out. Lizzie was on her feet again and beginning to look a little better, but Joseph was frightened the others would howl at him for his selfishness should he suggest the scullery maid walk the dog.

Beauty was not the quiet and chastened animal he had been before. He strutted and pranced, his mean little eyes flashing to right and left. Joseph let him off the leash in the Green Park and strolled over to where his friend, Luke, the first footman from next door, was taking the air.

"Got no work to do?" asked Joseph.

"Was sent over Kensington way with a note for Mr. Johnstone," said Luke, kicking the grass. "Thought I'd walk about a bit. Old Blenkinsop's waiting with piles o' silver for me to clean." Blenkinsop was the next door's butler. "Wot you a-doin' of?"

"Walking that dog," said Joseph. "Where's he gone, by the way? Oh, lor'!"

For Beauty was on the other side of the reservoir in full cry after an Irish wolfhound. The wolfhound was grabbed and rescued by its furious master, who held Beauty off with his whip until Joseph and Luke came running up. Joseph leashed Beauty and with many fulsome apologies tried to allay the wrath of the wolfhound's owner.

When all had quietened down again, Joseph glared down at Beauty and said to Luke, "Hold his leash. I'm going to give this pox of an animal a thrashing."

"Leave him be," said Luke, flushed with excitement. "Here, boy." He fished in a pocket of his livery and drew out a chocolate, which Beauty snapped up and then sat, panting for more.

"You lost your wits?" demanded Joseph furiously.

"Naw, that there h'animal's money, sacks and sacks of it."

"Garn," said Joseph, who had given up trying to be genteel in Luke's company.

"Streuth, swelp me if it ain't," said Luke. "This here dog is a fighter and there's a dog-fight over on the Surrey side. Champion Killer takes all-comers."

"What's in it for us?"

"A purse of fifty pound, not to mention what we could pick up on side bets. This dog don't look like much. But see the teeth on him!"

Joseph bent down to inspect Beauty's teeth, and Beauty snarled horribly and backed away.

"It's difficult," said Joseph, straightening up. "Fact is, that animal's taken agin me. It'd savage me before we got it over Westminster Bridge."

"Joseph!" called a female voice.

"Lizzie," said Joseph gloomily. "Always following me around."

But the change in Beauty was instant. He wagged his tail furiously and strained at the leash.

Luke stroked his chin thoughtfully. "There's one person he likes," he said. "Let him off the leash."

Once more Joseph slipped the leash, and Beauty bounded towards Lizzie, uttering ecstatic yips, and then leapt up and down trying to lick her face.

"Good dog," said Lizzie. "Now, lie down."

Beauty immediately lay down on the grass and stared up at her with adoring eyes.

"Mr. Rainbird sent me out to get some fresh air, Mr. Joseph," said Lizzie shyly. "Good afternoon, Mr. Luke."

She dropped the other footman a curtsy.

"I've got something private to say to Joseph," said Luke. "Could you please take the dog for a little walk, Lizzie? He seems to like you."

Lizzie nodded and took the leash from Joseph and set off down the park with Beauty prancing at her heels.

"Now, if we could get Lizzie to come along with us," said Luke, "we'd see some famous sport."

"She'd never take mistress's pet to a dog fight," exclaimed Joseph.

"She wouldn't know till we got there," said Luke impatiently, "and then she would be part of the plot and she'd have to keep her trap shut."

"But how can I get the evening off . . . let alone take Lizzie with me? How can you get off?"

"I'll spin Blenkinsop some yarn or other. Now, look here, you told me they fuss a lot over that scullery maid and that she's been ill and caused a fuss what with getting her cordials and a new bed and all."

"Yes, I told you that."

"Why not tell Rainbird we're taking her out for a little walk and we may as well take the dog. It's only the other side of the bridge. One ten-minute round and we'll run home."

"I dunno," said Joseph, looking worried.

"Fifty pounds, 'member, not to mention the bets."

Joseph made up his mind. "Very well," he said. "But I don't like tricking Lizzie."

"You spoony about her?"

"A scullery maid? Me?" demanded Joseph with awful hauteur. "I wouldn't lower meself."

Luke saw Lizzie standing a little way off, eyeing them wistfully. He called her over.

"Look, Lizzie," said Luke. "I've been hearing as how you've been ill."

Lizzie flushed with pleasure to think her adored Joseph had actually talked about her to his best friend.

"Well, see here," Luke went on heartily, "Joseph and I were thinking of taking a little stroll just over Westminster Bridge tonight and wondered if you would like to take the air with us. May as well take that dog along. It's one way of making sure the mistress and Mr. Rainbird give Joseph permission."

"Oh, I would love to go," said Lizzie, beginning to tremble with excitement. "D'ye think Mrs. Middleton will let me go, Joseph?"

Joseph frowned, thinking Lizzie was getting above herself. He liked her to call him "Mr. Joseph" in front of Luke.

"Matters will be arranged," said Joseph loftily. He moved off with Luke, and Lizzie followed behind, leading Beauty.

Miss Metcalf was delighted when Rainbird appeared before her to request permission that Lizzie and Joseph should be allowed time off that evening to take the air and to walk Beauty. Harriet had secured tickets for the playhouse for herself and the girls. She always felt guilty about having a pet such as Beauty and could only be glad that these town servants appeared to have accepted the dog's existence without question. Much as she longed to take Beauty for walks herself, she did not want to bring the censure of the ton down upon her head and therefore spoil Annabelle's and Sarah's chances of a successful Season.

And Beauty *was* a peculiar-looking pet. The aristocracy kept monkeys, parrots, or pugs as pets, for in these harsh times only the very rich could afford the luxury of being sentimental about animals. Dogs such as Beauty were meant to earn their keep by either ratting or turning a spit. Not wanting to be damned as eccentric, Harriet tried most of the time to hide her real love for the animal.

Lizzie dressed in her best gown and brushed her hair until she had nearly restored it to its usual shiny lustre. She tied up her tresses with one much-prized scarlet silk ribbon and polished the tin buckles on her shoes. But so great was her excitement that a hectic colour rose in her cheeks and she nearly burst into tears when Alice, Jenny, and Mrs. Middleton started to debate the wisdom of her going out at all.

But soon the magic moment actually arrived and she was out in Clarges Street flanked by Luke and Joseph, surely, thought Lizzie proudly, two of the most handsome men in London.

To her surprise, Luke led the way down to the mews at the bottom of Clarges Street. He said Joseph had suggested they hire a gig for an hour, as Lizzie might find a walk too much in her frail condition, and Lizzie looked up at Joseph with eyes like stars, amazed that her hero should go to so much trouble to look after her.

No sooner were they in Lambeth Mews than Beauty took exception to the horse when it was being harnessed to the gig and tried to savage it. Luke cried to Joseph to hold Beauty, and, whipping out a piece of thin rope, bound up the dog's jaws.

"Must you do that?" cried Lizzie. "He looks so distressed." Lizzie did not care much for animals one way or another. She petted the kitchen cat because it was Joseph's, but fondness for animals was a sophisticated luxury she could not afford. The Moocher earned his keep by being a mouser par excellence. A dog such as Beauty, who lolled around doing nothing, was a disgrace. But Lizzie adored the gentle and sweet Miss Metcalf, and there was something almost human about the panic in Beauty's wildly rolling little eyes.

Beauty was thrown on the floor of the gig. Lizzie sat beside Joseph and Luke sat in front, holding the reins.

Lizzie began to feel a twinge of unease. Both Luke and Joseph smelled strongly of spirits and had a strung-up air about them. They appeared to have forgotten that the outing was in her honour, and when Luke swung the gig round into Piccadilly and Lizzie was thrown against Joseph's shoulder, the footman pushed her roughly away.

When they got out onto Westminster Bridge, it was to find it crammed with traffic. Everyone appeared to be going to Vauxhall Gardens. Down on the floor, Beauty let out a low whine of distress. He was feeling sick with the stop, start, and stop-again movement of the gig, and Luke had bound the rope about his jaws very tightly.

"Please may I unmuzzle Beauty?" said Lizzie. "He is very quiet now."

"Suppose we'd better keep him in plump currant," said Luke, turning round and winking at Joseph. "He can't do anything, not now we're in the carridge."

Lizzie untied the rope from about Beauty's mouth. Beauty shifted restlessly and growled.

"Quiet," said Joseph. Beauty looked up at Joseph with hate in his eyes. He blamed Joseph for his own discomfort, and the footman smelled faintly of cat. Beauty bared his teeth.

Joseph leaned down to cuff the dog, and Beauty seized his black velvet sleeve and tore savagely. Joseph let out a scream of outrage.

Beauty leapt from the slowly moving gig and vanished into the crowd, his leash trailing behind him.

Luke swore and swung the gig across the traffic to try to follow the dog. There was a sickening scratching sound as the gig slid along the side of an aristocratic carriage, leaving a long score in the varnish.

"Oh, Gawdstreuth!" swore Luke, who recognised not only the carriage but also the choleric face glaring out of the open window at him.

It was his master, Lord Charteris.

"What are you doing here?" screamed his lordship. "No, don't answer. Bound to be a lie. Tell Blenkinsop to take the money out of your wages to pay for the revarnishing of my carriage and present yourself before me tomorrow in my study at two o'clock in the afternoon."

Before Luke could say anything, Lord Charteris slammed up the glass and rapped on the roof with his cane as a signal to his coachman to drive on.

"Well, that's that," said Luke, swinging the carriage round. "I told old Blenkinsop I was going to see my granny in Euston what's supposed to be dying."

"And he swallowed that?" exclaimed Joseph. "You told Blenkinsop last year when we went to Ascot that you was at your gran's funeral."

"Stow it," muttered Luke miserably.

"We can't go away and leave Beauty," cried Lizzie.

"Oh, yes we can," said Joseph savagely. "You'll never catch him now. Me, I don't care if he's drownded."

Lizzie leapt from the gig, stumbling slightly as she regained her balance on the road, and then ran off into the crowd.

"Let her go," said Luke. "She won't find the dog, and it ain't too far for her to get back."

Joseph felt he ought to get down and go after Lizzie. But Joseph considered small feet aristocratic and was wearing his best shoes, which were two sizes too small for him.

His toes throbbed and ached. He would have to tell some lies when he got back. But Lizzie would not let him down. She never did.

Lizzie ran to one of the bays on the bridge and looked across to Stangate on the south side of the River Thames. Sure enough, there was Beauty. Two youths caught at his leash and began to drag him away. With a cry of alarm, Lizzie set off running again. She ran down along Stangate, along Fore Street, until, in the fading light, she saw Beauty ahead, still being dragged along by the youths.

Beauty had had enough. He had just recovered from the shock of having found himself dragged roughly along. Enough was enough. He turned about and sank his teeth into the ankle of one of the youths, who let out a scream of pain and dropped Beauty's leash. Beauty smelled trees and flowers and grass, all the scents of the country, all the scents of home. He scampered off as fast as he could, straight past the turnstile at the entrance to Vauxhall Gardens, and ran into the trees and lay down, luxuriating in his freedom.

Lizzie, who had seen him disappear into the gardens, decided there was nothing else for it but to follow him in.

Vauxhall Pleasure Gardens did not normally open up until May, but they had been opened early for this one night to celebrate the retiral of that famous ballad singer, Mrs. Carlise.

The Gardens were a quadrangular grove of approximately twelve acres of closely planted trees. Four principal alleys, bisected formally by lesser roads at right angles, ran through the trees. In the clearances, there were Grecian columns, alcoves, theatres, temples, an orchestra, and an area for dancing. The Gardens were unusual in that they cut across class lines, being frequented by the ordinary people as well as the aristocracy.

Lizzie felt through the slit in the side of her gown to the pocket in her petticoat and extracted a shilling Rainbird had given her. Once inside, she discovered all the disadvantages of being an unescorted female. Every time she strayed from the path to search in the trees for Beauty, she was pursued by some boozy buck and had to fight and claw her way to safety. She tried calling "Beauty," but a chorus of bloods sent up such a mocking chorus that she decided to search in silence. She was beginning to feel dizzy and faint. Fear for Harriet's pet combined with the light comfort of her new shoes had, up till that moment, leant her feet wings, but now her legs trembled and she blundered about in the darkness, thinking every moving shape was the lost dog.

Beauty had gone exploring. Some Cit had stolen his leash and he was now enjoying the comfort of being able to run about without it becoming caught on the bushes. His stomach gave a rumble. He sniffed the air. Floating towards him came the delicious aroma of Westphalia ham. He followed his nose until he came out in a clearing.

In front of him was a semi-circle of boxes filled with ladies and gentleman seated at table, enjoying an al fresco supper.

Then Beauty's beady eyes focused on a couple in one of the lower boxes. He recognised the gentleman. Sure of his welcome as only a thoroughly spoilt animal can be, Beauty bounded forward with a glad little yip of delight.

The Marquess of Huntingdon was feeling jaded and weary. He began to think he might be destined to lead the life of a monk. Beside him, at a table in a box at Vauxhall, sat Belinda Romney. Her hair was pomaded to a high shine, and her eyes gleamed as green as the emeralds about her neck. Her shoulders were magnificent. The marquess looked at her with revulsion. He could never lie with her again. How many such full-blown roses had he gathered? He suddenly remembered, when he was still in petticoats, having stolen and eaten too many chocolates. His mother, unaware of his sin, had presented him with a chocolate, and he had turned green and rushed from the drawing room. He felt rather like that small boy now when he looked at Belinda.

Ever since the faithlessness of his late wife had proved to him that seeming purity and innocence could cover the heart of a harlot, he had preferred to take his pleasures with the Fashionable Impure. Among them, one was safe from disillusion.

He realised he would need to terminate his affair with Belinda. It would be costly—but only financially, not emotionally.

"Belinda, we have enjoyed a good liaison—" he began.

"And would it enjoy it better," said Belinda, "if perhaps we could eat. Are you going to carve that ham, or is it solely for ornament?"

"My apologies." The marquess rose and went to the tiny carving table and picked up the long sharp knife and carving fork. He had just sliced several wafers of ham and was arranging them on a plate, when all at once he felt Harriet Metcalf's arms about his neck and Harriet's lips against his own. The fantasy was so real that he felt a surge of sweetness coursing through his veins.

He was unaware of what was going on, oblivious to the fact that Belinda was cringing back with a scream as Beauty leapt into the marquess's recently vacated chair and leered amiably at the laughing crowd below.

The marquess absentmindedly slid the plate of ham in front of Beauty.

The vision of Harriet faded.

He blinked. Belinda was making gargling noises and pointing at Beauty, who was tucking into the plate of ham.

The marquess recognised Beauty. "What are you doing here?" he asked.

"Do you expect the dog to reply?" demanded Belinda shrilly. "That is the animal that attacked me in the Park."

"It's Harriet Metcalf's dog," said the marquess, hanging over the edge of the box, his eyes raking the crowd.

"Indeed!" Belinda's eyes narrowed into slits. She had found out Harriet's name at the Phillips' ball, being anxious to discover the identity of the fair charmer who appeared to be seducing her lover away from her.

"Huntingdon," said Belinda sharply, "get rid of that animal."

"In a minute," he said, his eyes still searching the crowd. "I'm looking for Miss Metcalf."

"Oooh!" In a flaming temper, Belinda brought her fan down hard on Beauty's narrow head. Beauty seized the fan and crunched up the tortoiseshell sticks and spat the wreckage on the table.

Belinda spied one of her admirers in the watching, jeering, laughing crowd below. "Huntingdon," she said, "an you do not do something about that cur, I shall leave you."

The marquess did not reply, for he had just spied Lizzie.

"Why, there's that scullery maid. What is her name? Ah. Lizzie . . . Lizzie!" he called loudly.

Lizzie looked up and saw not only the marquess but Beauty, who was standing on the table, lapping up the contents of a bowl of rack punch.

As Lizzie reached the box, Beauty slowly keeled over and fell down in a drunken stupor on the table and began to snore.

"I shall take him," said Lizzie eagerly. "I am so sorry, my lord, but I searched and searched . . ." She picked up the dog's heavy, inert body and then stood swaying, her face as white as paper.

The marquess caught her about the waist and called to Belinda. "Help me with her. I cannot hold both dog and girl."

Belinda, with a look of jealous rage, said, "Then I

suggest you send for Miss Metcalf." She tripped lightly from the box and disappeared on the arm of her admirer, a Mr. Lacey, who, seeing her fury with the marquess, had been waiting hopefully below the box.

The marquess heaved Lizzie into a chair, picked Beauty up by his collar and threw him under the table, soaked his handkerchief in iced water, and applied it to the maid's temples. Lizzy tried to struggle up, but he held her down with a firm hand.

"Where is your mistress?" he asked.

"Miss Metcalf is at the play, my lord. You see, it all started when I met our footman, Joseph, in the Green Park. . . ."

The marquess listened until she had finished her story. Then he said, "You are fortunate, young Lizzie, in that I am on the point of returning to the West End, so you may travel in my carriage as far as Clarges Street."

He tried to revive Beauty, without success, so he threw the inebriated dog around his neck like some horrible sort of tippet and led the way to his carriage. Many of the notables stared to see the great Marquess of Huntingdon handing what was obviously a servant of the lowest sort into his carriage and wearing what looked like a dead dog about his neck.

The marquess treated his servants with the same detached courtesy as he treated most members of the ton. So on the journey back, he encouraged Lizzie to talk about herself and pointed out various notables to her just as if he were entertaining a young debutante.

That carriage drive meant very little to the marquess, but it meant all the world to Lizzie. She spent most of her life below ground, although Rainbird was very generous about letting her go out for walks, and she felt she had been transported to another world. The air was warm and sweet. The lamps on Westminster Bridge flickered in their glass shields. For the first time in her life, Lizzie began to wonder whether she would always be a scullery maid, or whether there was not some road up for her—some road which would lead to carriage rides and bring her into a world where she would be treated with the gentle, thoughtful courtesy she was experiencing at that moment.

"I do not know why Joseph and Luke should want to take me and the dog out in a gig," she said timidly.

"My dear young lady," said the marquess, "when two young men show a sudden desire to rush a dog over to the Surrey side, it usually means they plan to enter that dog in a fight."

"They would never do that," gasped Lizzie.

"There is a lot of money to be gained. Do not be too hard on them."

Lizzie digested this in silence. Joseph had always seemed to Lizzie the epitome of everything that was gentlemanly, even though he did do such dreadful things. But here she was with a real gentleman, and he did not jeer at her or find her silly. When he swung off the bridge, she swayed towards him and without taking his eyes from the road, he put out a hand to support her. Joseph would have thrust her away.

"I do not suppose your mistress will be returned home," said the marquess.

"No, my lord," said Lizzie. "I shall take the dog down to the kitchen and . . . and . . . make as little fuss as possible." She looked at him anxiously.

"Yes, my child," he said, "you may rest assured that I shall leave all the talking to you. You are wondering what lies you will have to tell in order to support the footman's story."

This was exactly what Lizzie had been wondering, and she looked at him in awe.

But alas for Joseph. He was already in deep trouble before Lizzie arrived at Number 67. Rainbird had been horrified when Joseph had returned alone. In vain had the footman blustered and tried to make light of it. Rainbird had heard of the departure in the gig. Why rent a gig when the purpose of the outing had been to walk with Lizzie? And what had Luke to do with it?

At last, backed up against the kitchen wall, faced by a furious butler and cook, Joseph blurted out the truth.

"You heartless man," cried Jenny. "Poor little Lizzie. She thought you were doing it all for her. Oh, what will the mistress say?"

"Nothing. For all of us must go and find that dog as well as Lizzie if it takes all night," said Rainbird. "Mrs. Middleton, you had best stay with Dave to mind the house while the rest of us go out."

The searchers were just emerging from the basement when a high-perched phaeton rolled to a stop in front of the house, and they stood open-mouthed as the Marquess of Huntingdon jumped down and helped Lizzie to alight. Then the marquess picked up Beauty from the floor of the carriage. It was then they all turned and saw Harriet Metcalf standing on the step.

There had been a riot at the play, a not infrequent occurrence these days, because the managers of the play-house had raised the price of the seats and the public had once again taken their nightly revenge.

Lord Vere had been at the play and had been wonderful in extricating the ladies from the riot and bearing them home. When he had left, Annabelle and Sarah had said they were going to bed to have an early night, and Harriet had been sitting in the front parlour reading a book when she had heard the noise of the marquess's arrival.

Now she stood, the light evening breeze lifting the errant strands of her fair hair, which always escaped from their moorings no matter how expert the hairdressing, and saw the marquess with Beauty lying in his arms.

She thought Beauty was dead. And on top of that shattering thought came the realisation that she must not cry or make a scene in front of the servants over the death of a mongrel. Amazed at the steadiness of her own voice, she said, "Is he dead?"

"Dead drunk," said the marquess.

Harriet ran forward and pried up one of Beauty's eyes. He gave a faint snore and stirred in the marquess's arms. "Thank the Lord," said Harriet under her breath. Then she saw Lizzie.

"Please tell me what happened?" she said.

The marquess nodded his head towards Lizzie as a signal that the scullery maid was to give the explanation. Lizzie looked at Joseph, and Joseph threw her a pleading look.

"I am afraid your dog ran away, Miss Metcalf. I should have waited for Joseph to come with me, but I chased after the dog and found him eventually in Vauxhall Gardens. His lordship was kind enough to take me home."

Harriet became aware of all the faces at the windows along the street.

"It is most good of you, my lord," she said. "May I offer you some refreshment?"

The marquess's intelligence prompted him to refuse. His emotions screamed to him to accept. His emotions won.

"Thank you," he said. "Perhaps one of your servants could look after my horses?"

He followed Harriet into the house, still carrying Beauty.

"May I put this dog down somewhere, ma'am?" he asked plaintively. "I don't know how that little servant girl of yours managed even to try to lift him. He's deuced heavy."

"Certainly," said Harriet. "Place him in front of the fire. Sit down, my lord, and tell me how my poor Beauty comes to be drunk."

The marquess placed Beauty down on the carpet and then sat down in a chair facing Harriet. Harriet blushed slightly and would not meet his eyes. She was already regretting her invitation. For, at the playhouse, before the riot started, she had been overcome with such physical longing for him that she had felt haunted and then had thought miserably that London must be turning her mind to carnal thoughts and herself into a strumpet.

"I was at Vauxhall," said the marquess, "at supper, when suddenly I looked round and there was your dog, sitting at table, with a knife and fork in his paws, demolishing wafers of ham."

"What really happened?" asked Harriet. "Thank you, Rainbird. Put the tray down there and we shall serve ourselves."

"He did help himself to a plate of ham, Miss Metcalf, and then Lizzie came rushing up and nearly fainted, by which time Beauty had had his snout in the punch bowl and had passed out."

Harriet poured a glass of wine for him and then one for herself.

"My poor Beauty," said Harriet. "I am afraid he is not a very well-disciplined dog."

The marquess thought that was putting it mildly, but he politely said nothing and studied her instead. A branch of candles on the mantelpiece was gilding her hair. Her gown was of a soft blue material, the low neck being edged with a fall of lace.

"I must reward Lizzie in some way," said Harriet. "It was brave of her to go looking for Beauty alone."

"Perhaps braver than you realise, ma'am. Vauxhall Gardens is no place for an unattended young lady. Imagine it. Her searching in the dark, going out of her wits with worry. She is a thoroughly nice child."

"Perhaps money . . ." ventured Harriet.

"Money is not the answer to everything," said the

marquess. "If you give her money, she will no doubt share it with the other servants. You have a basement full of Jacobites. One has only to see them altogether for even a second to realise they have formed themselves into some democratic sort of clan. I felt I was meeting Lizzie's family when I returned, rather than her superiors."

"Not much of a family when they allow the child to sleep on a damp mattress on the scullery floor," said Harriet.

"It must be a hard life for them," mused the marquess. "They appear to be servants only for each Season, rather than attached to some great household where they are employed all the year round. I do not suppose they are paid very much when the Season is over. It would explain their indifference to Lizzie's sleeping quarters. Only people like us who are well-fed can afford the luxury of sentimental feelings for waifs . . . or dogs."

"I have no money," retorted Harriet defensively, "but Beauty, at one time, was the only friend I had and I was glad to share my food with him."

"To return to the subject of little Lizzie. Education for such as she is more valuable than gold. With a little training and learning she could aspire to be a housemaid and then perhaps a lady's maid."

"That is a very good idea," said Harriet warmly. "I shall teach her myself."

He smiled at her suddenly, liking her earnestness for Lizzie's welfare, liking the fall of her gown and the soft sweetness of her voice.

Some devil prompted Harriet to say, "I trust your companion at Vauxhall was not too overset by the behaviour of my vulgar dog?"

"Yes," said the marquess, his face going a polite blank, "she was."

Harriet should have realised the marquess would naturally not be attending Vauxhall on his own. But she had hoped he had been there with a gentleman friend. Only because, she told herself severely, she wished the best for Sarah.

But a shadow crossed her face, and she finished her glass of wine very quickly and looked pointedly at the clock.

The marquess put down his glass and rose to his feet. Harriet rose as well and dropped him a curtsy by way of underlining the fact she expected him to take his leave.

He raised her hand to his lips and smiled down into her eyes.

Harriet snatched her hand away and buried it in the folds of her skirt.

His face flamed at the insult.

"You are so . . . practised in the art of flirtation, my lord," said Harriet, "and I am not."

"No," agreed the marquess. "No one could accuse you of even trying to practise the art of being polite. Good evening."

Sadly, Harriet watched him go and then listened until the last rumble of his carriage wheels had faded on the night. Lord Vere did not prompt such bad behaviour in her. She sat down on the floor beside Beauty and stroked his rough, shaggy fur. "What is happening to me, Beauty?" she asked.

But Beauty's only answer was a drunken snore.

Chapter
Seven

Do you know, Carter, that I can actually write my
name in the dust on the table?
Faith, Mum, that's more than I can do. Sure,
there's nothing like education, after all.

—Punch

Rainbird descended to the servants' hall the next day with the news that Lizzie was to be taught her letters by Miss Metcalf. Miss Metcalf intended to begin on the morrow by giving Lizzie half an hour of her time at ten-thirty in the morning.

"Reckon she deserves it," said Alice in her slow way. "I ain't much good when it comes to education, not me."

"Me neither," said Dave. "Why Liz?"

" 'Cos she's a brave girl, that's why," said Jenny, shooting a venomous look at Joseph. "See here, Lizzie, when we get that pub we're set on, you can keep the books and sit there like a lady."

"I could hae taught her," growled Angus MacGregor, the cook.

"Well, she probably wouldn't have larned much o' you," said Joseph. "You'd hehve shouted at her and hit her with the roasting spit if she hedn't hehve done what you said."

"We Scots are no' like you Sassenachs," said the cook. "There's hardly a bairn in the length and breadth of the country that doesn't know his letters."

"Don't be getting above yourself, Lizzie," said Mrs. Middleton.

"And pass on to us what she teaches you," said Alice. "We could have a school down here in the winter."

Education fever set in, and Rainbird promised to buy some secondhand primers for all of them.

Only Joseph sat a little apart, smarting both physically and mentally. He had had a hiding from Rainbird the evening before, but it was Lizzie's new attitude towards him that hurt the most.

Joseph had not realised how much he had come to take the little scullery maid's devotion for granted. Lizzie now barely looked at him.

Abovestairs, Harriet was breakfasting with Sarah and Annabelle, giving them a carefully edited version of the previous night's happenings. Caution prompted her not to say she had entertained the marquess. Although she was sure dear Sarah would understand, the girl might be upset nonetheless at missing a chance of spending further time in his company.

If only there were two Lord Veres, thought Harriet.

The rest of the day passed pleasantly enough. Lord Vere called and chatted to Sarah and Annabelle for quite half an hour. Then they went out to the opera, where he had secured them a box. There was no sign of the Marquess of Huntingdon.

Harriet took her charges during the following week to balls and routs and parties. The Season was rushing upon them; the pace becoming hectic. The marquess did not put in an appearance at any of the events. Sarah began to show signs of turning petulant and kept asking Harriet sweetly if she had said something to offend the handsome lord.

Harriet was just beginning to wonder whether to admit

to Sarah that she had in fact been very rude indeed to Lord Huntingdon when Lord Vere brought him back into their lives.

He said the marquess had proposed a carriage ride. Lord Vere had discovered the marquess had been away visiting his country estate, and the marquess had surprised him on his return by suggesting the outing.

Lord Vere was by now hopelessly in love with Harriet and had decided to propose. He did not want his friend, however, to suspect any of this, for he feared the marquess might steal a march on him.

Having accepted the invitation, Harriet then began to worry about the wisdom of going along herself. She felt sure something would prompt her to annoy the marquess, he would be furious, and Sarah's hopes would be dashed. Harriet was just wondering what to do when Miss Josephine Spencer arrived at Number 67. Harriet was delighted to see her. It transpired that Miss Spencer had come to Town to stay with an elderly relative in Lincoln's Inn Fields. Harriet sat down and regaled her friend with all the things that had happened since she had come to London.

Miss Spencer heard her out in silence and then said, "You are sure that this Lord Vere and Lord Huntingdon are not interested in you, rather than in the twins?"

"No, of course not," said Harriet. "I do not have a dowry. But there is something I have not told you, Josephine. I say the most terrible things to Huntingdon and have given him quite a disgust of me, so I am very obviously not the reason for the outing tomorrow. But I am worried I might say something wrong—and Sarah would never forgive me. She is quite taken with the marquess. In fact," said Harriet with a burst of candour, "any woman would be taken with him. He is devastatingly handsome and . . . and he has a sweet smile. But he is a rake."

"Aren't they all," said Miss Spencer cynically.

"I do wish I had someone to send along tomorrow instead of me."

"I'll go," said Miss Spencer promptly, "provided you are sure it is not you the gentlemen are after."

"Of course not!"

"Don't sound surprised. I would have thought . . . well, never mind. What excuse shall I give them?"

But before Harriet could reply, Rainbird entered, obviously wishing to speak to her, and then stopped when he saw Miss Spencer, because Joseph had let her in and, thinking she was an old frump of no consequence, had not bothered to tell the butler of her arrival.

"Yes, Rainbird?" asked Harriet.

"It is a private matter, ma'am," said Rainbird.

"You may speak about it now, if you wish," said Harriet. "Miss Spencer is an old friend and knows all my affairs."

Rainbird took a deep breath and plunged in. He had learned earlier from Harriet of the proposed outing to Richmond, and, since his services would not be required on the morrow, he wished to take a day's leave to go to Brighton to see "a very old friend."

The butler's heart had been aching for Felice, the French lady's maid. He had tried to school himself to wait until the end of the Season when he would be free, but he was frantically worried that she might be contemplating marriage to some burgher.

Miss Metcalf studied him so long in silence that Rainbird began to fear he had offended her. Then she surprised him by saying, "Brighton. I have never seen the sea. Also, I am worried about little Lizzie. Perhaps we all need fresh air. Hire a large travelling carriage, Rainbird, and we shall all go."

Rainbird tried to keep his features correctly immobile, but his comedian's face radiated happiness.

"Thank you, Miss Metcalf," he said. "I shall inform the

rest of the staff. We have the pot boy, Dave, who can stay to mind the house."

"I do not think that would be fair to Dave," said Harriet. "We will make sure all the shutters are closed and the doors locked and barred."

When Rainbird had left, Miss Spencer said thoughtfully, "That is a most attractive man, your butler."

"Rainbird?"

"Yes, Rainbird. He has a clever face and a good body and his legs are all his own. No false calves there."

"Wait until you meet the Marquess of Huntingdon." Harriet laughed. "Baroness Villiers, who is quite a grim old dowager, told me without a smile on her face that Huntingdon's legs were the 'talk of Europe.'"

Miss Spencer smiled, although her brain was working furiously. She wondered whether Harriet was in love with this marquess.

Sarah and Annabelle were delighted with the new arrangements. Both were beginning to feel Harriet was much too pretty to have around, and a dragon like Miss Spencer as chaperone would certainly not distract any gentleman from their own charms.

Privately, they laughed and giggled over the idea of Harriet going off to Brighton with a parcel of servants. "And mark my words," said Sarah, wiping her streaming eyes, "she'll take that wretched smelly dog with her, and it will savage everything on the Brighton road."

"You know, Sis," said Annabelle, "have you noticed that although Harriet sits against the wall at balls and parties just as she ought, the gentlemen do seem to show a marked degree of interest in her?"

"Of course they do, stoopid," said Sarah. "How else can they get introductions to us?"

Down in the servants' hall, excitement was reaching fever pitch. The only one unaffected was Emily, who absented herself more and more from the servants' hall. She had said she was always with her young mistresses, as they changed their gowns at least six times a day, but Jenny said that Mary, the housemaid next door, had seen Emily walking through Shepherd Market talking to a fashionable lady. Emily surprised them all by saying she did not want to go. The Misses Hayner were not leaving until ten in the morning, whereas Miss Metcalf and the servants would be leaving at dawn. She would be expected to prepare the ladies for their outing and someone should be indoors to guard the house, she added righteously. Lizzie felt she would die from happiness. The fact that Emily was not to join them was all that was needed to guarantee a day of pure pleasure. Long after Harriet, Sarah, and Annabelle had retired for the night, the servants were awake, brushing down their best clothes and polishing their shoes. Rainbird had hired a spanking travelling carriage from the best livery stable in Town. He hoped Miss Metcalf would not be shocked at the expense.

Everyone in their various ways prayed for good weather. Lizzie turned so white with excitement at the thought of seeing the sea that she was sent to lie down. She lay on her new bed, hardly able to luxuriate in its comfort as she usually did, because she was afraid that something terrible would happen to prevent them going.

But the morning dawned clear and fair, and at first light they were all piling aboard. Even Beauty looked excited, having recovered from his excesses at Vauxhall. With his mistress by him, he looked a meek and servile dog.

The sight of the Moocher skulking at the top of the kitchen steps made him try to break free, but a stern word from Harriet cowed him. Still, somewhere in the dim recesses of his mind, Beauty registered two facts—cat and kitchen.

Luke was gloomily polishing the brass on the door of Number 65. Why was that Joseph always saying what an unlucky house he worked in? Exciting things seemed to happen at Number 67. Who else ever got taken out for a day by their master or mistress? And what a set-up! What a spanking rig with four fifteen-mile-an-hour tits to pull it.

Gloomily waving his polishing rag in farewell, Luke watched them until the carriage had turned the corner into Piccadilly.

Mrs. Middleton, Jenny, Alice, and Lizzie rode inside with Harriet, while the menservants travelled on the roof.

Harriet had had a hard job hiding her alarm when Rainbird told her how much the carriage, coachman, and groom were going to cost, but she covered her dismay well. It was distressing to be always spending someone else's money. After some reflection, Harriet, who had been hoping to save as much of her own small income as possible, decided to dip into it to cover the costs of the outing. She apologised to Lizzie for the postponement of her lessons, promised to begin them on the following morning, and then settled down to enjoy the drive.

Mrs. Middleton asked Harriet if what the newspapers said was true and that the Prince of Wales planned to reconstruct the Marine Pavilion at Brighton and add Indian towers.

Harriet replied that from the gossip she had had of the other chaperones, she gathered that at the moment the Prince's taste was for chinoiserie, but she had heard that the Royal Stables and Riding House had been completed the year before and were said to be magnificent. The stables had an eighty-foot cupola and provided accommodation for forty-four horses in stalls going round the great circle of the interior, with harness rooms and grooms' quarters above the stalls. In the centre of the floor was a fountain for watering the horses. People had said the new buildings were in the Moslem-Indian style, so it could indeed be that the Prince was moving away from China.

Jenny, not used to talking freely to her betters, said

shyly that it now seemed certain that the Prince would become Regent. Harriet agreed and repeated more gossip.

Lizzie sat, drinking it all in. Miss Metcalf had an unaffected ease of manner to the servants which made them begin to relax, although all were careful not to overstep the mark and indulge in any familiarity.

It was all very exciting. They raced along the Brighton road, stopping at smart posting houses to change the horses and to take refreshment. Only Rainbird, as he efficiently dealt with ostlers and landlords along the way, began to doubt the wisdom of Miss Metcalf's treat. Dave and Joseph were so carried away by being treated like young gentlemen that both had started to swagger and put on airs—not unusual in Joseph's case, but worrying in Dave's.

Luxury bred discontent, as Rainbird well knew. They had all been guests at one of the previous tenants' weddings, but then they were still in the servants' quarters of a country house, and although they were not expected to work, they were still recognisable as servants.

But racing along down to Brighton on a sunny spring day and being waited on at the most expensive posting houses on the road was too heady a brew for such as young Dave. Rainbird could only be glad that dour Angus seemed indifferent to it all and that the women servants were behaving prettily.

The minute the first glimpse of the sea came into view, Rainbird ordered the coachman to stop. The ladies climbed down from inside.

Lizzie stood with her hands clasped, gazing at the great glittering blue expanse of the ocean, so elated, so moved, she began to cry a little with happiness and Harriet felt her own eyes brim over as well.

It was so wonderful, thought Harriet, to escape for a little with these oddly companionable servants, to leave the worries of Sarah and Annabelle in Miss Spencer's capable hands, and to forget about the disturbing and bewitching Marquess of Huntingdon for just one day.

When they arrived at Brighton, Harriet raised the trap and called to Rainbird to reserve a private parlour at some suitable inn where they would all meet for dinner at four o'clock. Harriet preferred the early country hour for dinner and found it hard to get used to the new London fashion of sitting down to dine as late as seven o'clock.

Rainbird decided on The Ship. He made arrangements for the stabling of the carriages and horses and then they all gathered about Harriet.

"Mr. Rainbird has someone he wishes to visit, but what would the rest of you like to do?" asked Harriet.

There was an awkward little silence while the servants looked at the butler, and the butler looked away.

In all the excitement of the outing, they had forgotten about the existence of Felice, that treacherous foreigner who had stolen poor Rainbird's heart away. Mrs. Middleton bent her head to hide the wounded expression in her eyes. She nourished secret hopes that one day, should they ever find themselves free from the shackles of service, Rainbird would marry her—for servants were not allowed to marry.

"I have heard tell o' a shop that sells all sorts of wondrous things made oot o' shells," said Angus MacGregor, breaking the silence.

"Lizzie will come with me," said Joseph, and it was obvious to all that the footman thought his great condescension worthy of applause. Lizzie looked decidedly uncomfortable.

Alice and Jenny were eager to stroll along by the sea and look for gallants. Dave wanted to play by the shore. Mrs. Middleton said quietly she would accompany Miss Metcalf.

"I think I would like to go with Mr. MacGregor and look at those shells," said Lizzie in a squeaky voice.

"Aye, weel, you're welcome tae come," said the cook, flashing a malicious look in Joseph's direction.

Joseph turned on his heel and flounced off without another word.

They all agreed to meet back at the inn at four. Harriet went off with Mrs. Middleton. Beauty was straining at his leash with excitement.

Rainbird set off alone. By the time he turned the corner into Lanceton Street where Felice lived, his heart was beating hard. If only he had had time to write to her.

Felice Laurent lived with a widow, a Mrs. Peters, at Number 11. It was a small villa, looking very much like the villas on either side. He stopped with his hand on the top of the low gate.

A lilac tree beside the little garden path was in bloom, its sweet scent mixed with the smell of salt from the sea.

He stood there for only a little, but to him it felt like an age before he could summon up courage to walk along the path and rap on the knocker.

There was a long silence, and then he heard someone moving towards the door.

It opened. He recognised Mrs. Peters, who stood there, blinking at him in the sunlight. She was the same as when he had last seen her, stout and middle-aged.

"Felice," said Rainbird. "I am come to see Felice."

"She does not live here any longer," said Mrs. Peters. "She's wed to a Mr. Malin, lives the other side, Bishop Row."

Rainbird stood very still. He saw the peeling paintwork on the door where it had been dried and blistered by the sun; he saw a caterpillar on a rose leaf on the flowerbed beside the half-open door; he felt the rush of warm wind on his cheek.

"Thank you," he said.

"It's Five Bishop Row. Number five," called Mrs. Peters to his retreating back.

Rainbird walked away as fast as he could.

Now where in Brighton, he wondered, *can a broken-hearted butler go to cry his eyes out in peace?*

Far away, at The Star and Garter in Richmond, two gentlemen were acting with great courtesy and charm. Never by one flicker of an eyelid did one of them show his surprise and dismay over the absence of Harriet Metcalf. Miss Spencer was to remember that day. She did not know what was wrong at the time. Everyone was behaving so perfectly. The Hayner girls were silly chits, but then so were any other debutantes that Miss Spencer had known. The gentlemen were amusing and charming. But underneath it all ran an undertow of emotion. Miss Spencer had an uneasy feeling that, behind his smiling eyes and amiable manner, the Marquess of Huntingdon was inwardly raging, but she decided that her fancies were caused by her disordered spleen. Both Sarah and Annabelle boasted large dowries, and men of the ton usually settled for birth and money in the ladies they chose to marry. So Miss Spencer was not surprised to observe that lovelight did not brighten either the marquess or Lord Vere's eyes.

She did feel that Sarah and Annabelle had made too much of a joke about "dear Harriet" choosing to go off with a parcel of servants for the day, a joke that they continued to enlarge on as the day wore on.

But perhaps, she, Josephine Spencer, was too nice in her ideas, for the gentlemen laughed heartily at all the girls' sallies and seemed to find nothing amiss.

Miss Spencer was impressed with Lord Huntingdon and could not help thinking it hard that poor Harriet did not have enough of a dowry to attract such a paragon. That some men might actually fall in love did not cross Miss Spencer's cynical mind. With the wars against Napoleon dragging on and on, prices had reached an all-time high, and everyone, no matter how high-minded, had become acutely conscious of the value of money.

The day was golden, the food was delicious, and she

was not to know that two gentlemen were thinking in their different ways that it was a perfect day for dalliance and romance. All it lacked was the lady.

Lord Vere decided to propose to Harriet as soon as possible. He felt he had waited for her a lifetime already. The marquess was wondering whether Miss Metcalf was cunningly aware of the force of her physical attractions and had deliberately stayed away to make him suffer. For to his surprise, he did suffer. He smiled at Sarah and all the while dreamed of strangling Harriet and kissing her at the same time.

The little staff from Number 67 Clarges Street had never before been so enthralled with their butler. Never before, all agreed, had Mr. Rainbird been so entertaining. He juggled oranges, he made hard-boiled eggs appear out of Dave's ears, and he presented Miss Metcalf with a bouquet of roses which he conjured out of the tails of his coat. He did cartwheels and handstands, all in the small confines of the parlour. Harriet laughed and clapped, amazed at the butler's talent, not knowing Rainbird had spent part of his youth as a fairground acrobat. And she could only be glad that the antics of this odd butler had dispelled a certain bad-tempered feeling which had hung in the air when the staff had first assembled for dinner.

Dave was looking bruised and bloody. Exalted with the thrill of being a guest for a day rather than a pot boy, he had swaggered up to three pages from the Marine Pavilion and had tried to patronise them. After looking at the wizened little Cockney in amazement, they had then set on him to bring him to a nice understanding of the importance of pages at the Prince of Wales's Marine Pavilion.

Joseph had been smarting over the snub Lizzie had delivered to him. He had gone for a lonely walk. It had not been at all the same without Lizzie trotting beside him, hanging on his every word.

Jenny and Alice had spent a pleasant hour with two

gallants, but that had all gone to underline the fact that they were servants and not free to have beaux or to marry. Discontent had set in, affecting even the normally placid and sunny Alice.

Mrs. Middleton and Harriet had arrived somewhat shaken. Beauty had behaved like his name until he had met a beribboned and prancing poodle and had tried to take it down a peg. The poodle belonged to a certain Lady Parsons, who had promptly gone into a spasm. The row had drawn a crowd, and Harriet had taken the coward's way out by seizing Beauty by the collar and dragging him away, consoling herself with the thought that Lady Parsons appeared to have a whole retinue of servants on hand to look after her.

Only the cook and the scullery maid had enjoyed a pleasant afternoon.

It was then that Rainbird had begun to clown. Harriet smiled as the little group of servants once more drew closely together, joined by common hilarity and common pride in their butler's prowess. Joseph was then sent to fetch his mandolin from the carriage and entertained them at the end of dinner with sentimental ballads.

The journey home was relaxed and pleasant. It was a tired but happy little party who finally debouched at Number 67 Clarges Street.

Sarah and Annabelle had already retired. Harriet was about to go upstairs to see if they were still awake so that she might find out how they had fared at Richmond when she saw two letters waiting for her on the silver salver on the hall table. Asking Rainbird to bring tea, she retired to the back parlour, which was more cluttered and cosy than the front one, and opened them up. Her heart beat hard as she read the contents.

Lord Vere wrote to say he would be calling on her at eleven o'clock in the morning because he wished to ask permission to pay his addresses.

The other was from the Marquess of Huntingdon. He

said he would call at two in the afternoon on the following day to discuss a serious matter concerning his future. He added lightly that at his great age it was time he settled down. Harriet felt a glow of triumph. Sarah and Annabelle would be engaged to two highly presentable men before the Season had even begun.

She ran up the stairs and knocked on Sarah's door and went in. The two girls were sitting in front of the fire. Harriet showed them both letters and hugged them warmly. Then she turned to Sarah.

"Are you sure, dear Sarah," she said, "that you consider it wise to accept such as the Marquess of Huntingdon? You are very young and his reputation—"

"Pooh!" laughed Sarah. "Turn down the biggest prize on the Marriage Mart? Do not be ridiculous, Harriet."

"Well . . . well . . . if that is how you feel," said Harriet. "I will rouse you, Annabelle, first. Wait in your room until I have given Lord Vere my permission and then I shall send for you."

Sarah and Annabelle threw their arms about her, calling her a clever puss and saying they were not very surprised because both gentlemen had all but declared themselves at Richmond.

Neither gentleman had done anything of the sort, but the twins were both possessed of an overweening vanity that made them quite capable of hearing compliments and proposals that had never been uttered.

Harriet went back downstairs to find Rainbird depositing the tea tray on the table. "Wonderful news," cried Harriet. "Lord Vere is calling tomorrow morning to ask my permission to pay his addresses to Annabelle, and in the afternoon, Lord Huntingdon will also call with a view to securing Sarah's hand in marriage."

"Felicitations," said Rainbird quietly. "On behalf of the servants, ma'am, we wish to thank you for a splendid day in Brighton."

"It was fun," said Harriet absentmindedly, her mind busy with plans. "Did you see your friend, Rainbird?"

"No, Miss Metcalf. It appears she has married and moved to another address. May I pour your tea?"

"Yes, Rainbird. Ask MacGregor to make some of those little caraway cakes. They are a great favourite of Lord Vere."

Rainbird bent over the tray and poured a cup of tea. A drop of moisture fell on Harriet's hand. She looked up quickly. The candle on the mantel lit only the table, leaving the butler's face in the shadows.

"Are . . . are you crying Rainbird?" asked Harriet.

The butler turned away, his back rigid as he made for the door.

"Will that be all, madam?"

"Yes, Rainbird," said Harriet sadly. "That will be all."

Poor Rainbird, thought Harriet. *He was crying.*

A great weight of depression settled on her, and she did not then realise that the idea of the Marquess of Huntingdon marrying Sarah was repugnant to her; she put all her sadness down to worry about her butler.

Chapter Eight

Let bygones be bygones:
Don't call me false, who owed not to be true;
I'd rather answer "No" to fifty Johns
Than answer "Yes" to you.

—Rossetti

Perhaps the day's events might have brought about the eternal ruin of Miss Harriet Metcalf's reputation had it not been for one simple little act of kindness on her part.

Despite the excitements that lay ahead, Harriet summoned Lizzie and began the girl's lessons. It was a relief to discover that the scullery maid was not entirely illiterate. She proved an apt pupil, and Harriet had hopes of seeing the girl able to read with ease before very long.

The previous day's outing had brought the roses back to Lizzie's pale cheeks, and the excitement of being treated to her gentle mistress's full attention made her eyes glow.

Harriet was also moved by her ugly pet's obvious devotion to the little servant. Beauty laid his head across the tin buckles of Lizzie's shoes and gazed up at her worshipfully from his small eyes.

Upstairs, the twins were already out of bed and sending Emily hither and thither to fetch ribbons and laces.

"Thought you wanted me to gossip about Miss Metcalf," said Emily as she heated the curling tongs on the spirit lamp.

"Not now, Emily," said Sarah. "Our country bumpkin has done amazing well for us. I have never been quite so in charity with her before. Do you say that she was running around Brighton with those servants?"

"They was all talking about it in the servants' hall last night," said Emily, picking up the tongs and a strand of Sarah's hair at the same time. "Seems she chatted away to them all just as if they was her equals and entertained them all to dinner at The Ship."

"It is the outside of enough," said Annabelle. "Do you hear, Sarah? Our money is being thrown into the laps of town servants who have probably already salted away a fortune."

Sarah shrugged. "Since she has been instrumental in securing Huntingdon for me, then she may take her pleasures belowstairs as much as she likes as far as I am concerned."

"Do you hear, Emily?" cried Annabelle. "How much my sister has changed! A forthcoming marriage soothes the savage breast wonderfully."

"But now they are all singing her praises," pointed out Emily. "It will be the harder now to turn them against her."

"You can always turn servants," said Sarah. "They do not really have minds of their own. But as of this moment we dote on our godmother. Do not wrench my hair, Emily. What has come over you?"

Harriet had put on her best morning gown to receive Lord Vere. It was of a misty-blue jaconet muslin made with a gored bodice and was finished with a tucker of fine embroidery. Over it she wore a cambric pelisse made with long sleeves. To add credence to her chaperone status, she had put on a dainty muslin cap. She thought it aged her nicely, unaware that the cap was vastly fetching, the almost transparent starched muslin sitting daintily on top of her blond head.

Although the day was warm, the heat had not yet permeated the building and so she had Joseph make up the fire with scented logs. Alice was sent to the market to bring bunches of daffodils and tulips to fill the vases in the front parlour.

Lord Vere arrived promptly. Harriet rose to meet him, looking at him with approval. For once he had forgone his usual Byronic style of dress and was wearing a blue swallow-tail coat and sporting a cravat of gigantic proportions.

He talked nervously of the weather and of how shattered he had been when she had failed to join the Richmond party.

Taking pity on his nervous condition, Harriet threw him a teasing look and said, "I am sure we could chat with greater ease if you unburdened yourself."

Wild hope gleamed in Lord Vere's eyes. To Harriet's amazement, he threw himself down on his knees in front of her.

"Love has taken away my courage," he said. "You are all the world to me, Miss Metcalf. Pray give me the very great honour of being allowed to call you mine."

Harriet sat very still, looking down at him, her blue eyes wide with shock.

At last she cleared her throat nervously and said, "Lord Vere, I cannot have heard you aright. I understood from your letter you wished to ask my permission to pay your addresses to Annabelle."

"Annabelle!" exclaimed Lord Vere, clutching Harriet's little hands in a painful grasp. "How could you think such a thing? It is you I love. I love you to distraction."

Harriet tugged miserably at her hands until he

released them. She stood up and Lord Vere stumbled to his feet as well.

"Lord Vere," said Harriet wretchedly, "if I have done anything, said anything unwittingly to encourage you in the belief that my affections were engaged, then I am truly sorry. I am in London solely in the position of chaperone to the Misses Hayner. I have no dowry and therefore I could not possibly believe any gentleman would wish to propose to me."

"But your lack of dowry does not matter," cried Lord Vere. "Miss Metcalf . . . sweet Harriet . . . please accept my proposal."

"I cannot," said Harriet, looking sadly at his face, thinking how very young he looked, although she knew him to be older than herself. "I had not thought of marriage for myself."

"Then I may hope? When this Season is over . . . ?"

"No, my lord," said Harriet firmly, although she felt a lump rising in her throat. "I am afraid there is no hope."

He seized her hands again and kissed them passionately and turned and ran from the room.

Sarah and Annabelle, who had been listening at the door, fell back just in time. So great was his distress that he did not even see them. The twins scampered upstairs to Annabelle's room.

"*Well!*" said Sarah, slamming the door. "Did you ever?"

Two bright spots of red burned in Annabelle's cheeks. "She has done it again," she hissed. "The lying, scheming jade."

"Why on earth did she refuse him?" asked Sarah.

"Because she is after your marquess, that's why."

But Sarah's vanity remained intact. "You imagined Lord Vere was after you, Annabelle. But there is one thing I know, Lord Huntingdon wishes to make me his own."

"Oh, really?" said Annabelle, quite animated with rage and venom, "Just you wait until two o'clock!"

"Shhh!" said Sarah. "Here she comes."

Annabelle picked up a book, and Sarah picked up a piece of sewing.

When Harriet came slowly into the room, the girls looked neat, calm, and maidenly.

"I am so sorry, Annabelle," said Harriet wretchedly. "He does not wish to propose to you."

"Then why did he write such a letter?" demanded Annabelle, keeping her eyes fastened on her book.

"He—Lord Vere, that is—was under the false idea that I, of all people, would welcome his advances. I refused, of course. Oh, my dear girls," said Harriet, her eyes filling with tears, "after all my hopes for you!"

"There is still Huntingdon," pointed out Sarah, with a malicious look at her sister.

"So there is," said Harriet, brightening. Her face fell again. "But Lord Vere was so suitable for Annabelle."

Annabelle composed herself and raised her eyes. "Do not fret, dear Harriet," she said. "The Season has not begun, and I was only going to accept Lord Vere for his title. My affections were not seriously engaged."

"Oh, you best of girls," said Harriet, giving her a hug. "You have no idea how much better I feel. Sarah, I shall send Rainbird for you directly when Lord Huntingdon asks my permission."

"How too vastly touching," sobbed Annabelle as soon as the door had closed behind Harriet. "I could not bear to let her see how badly my sensibilities have been wounded. I could strangle her!"

"Gently, Sis, only think what beaux I can find you when I am the Marchioness of Huntingdon."

Lord Huntingdon had come to the momentous decision to marry Harriet Metcalf after that dreadful outing to

Richmond. He and Gilbert, Lord Vere, had not discussed it, or the absence of Harriet Metcalf. The marquess had taken his leave of Lord Vere as soon as possible. He wanted to be alone to turn over the problem in his mind at his leisure.

Harriet had got under his skin. He had thought of nothing and no one else while he had sat listening to the trite chatter of those Hayner girls. His face felt stiff with smiling. He was sure he would not be causing any serious damage to Gilbert's heart. Lord Vere had seemed perfectly happy with the twins and had not asked after Harriet once.

That Harriet might refuse his offer never once crossed the marquess's mind. He knew his worth. He was rich, titled, and neither a cripple nor did he have a squint. No woman in her right mind would turn him down, particularly a penniless one.

As he walked along to Clarges Street, he did not notice that clouds had covered the sun, or feel the chill breath of the rising wind on his cheek. He was wrapped in dreams of how first overawed, then grateful Harriet Metcalf would be.

Harriet's experience with Lord Vere had somewhat dimmed the day for her, and it was a sedate little lady who rose to meet the marquess when he was ushered in.

He refused refreshment, wanting to get out the proposal that was burning in his mind. She looked so delectable. Her lips were soft and pink. He wondered how old she was. She had said something about her parents dying a certain time ago. She must be in her middle twenties, and yet she looked fresh and young and virginal.

But Harriet did not feel it necessary to encourage him to get his request to pay his addresses to Sarah over and done with. Unlike Lord Vere, he did not look in the slightest nervous. In fact, she thought he looked extremely handsome. His cravat was snowy perfection, and he wore his morning clothes with an air. His hessian boots shone like black glass. His chestnut hair gleamed with threads of gold. It was very thick and had a natural curl.

He smiled at Harriet suddenly—a warm, tender, and seductive smile. She felt the hot colour rising in her cheeks and wished he were not quite so attractive.

"Well, Miss Metcalf," he said, after the topic of the weather had been thoroughly exhausted, "you know why I am come."

"Yes, my lord," said Harriet calmly. He looked at her a little surprised. He would have considered it more in character if Harriet had looked a little flustered or nervous. But the wide blue eyes that met his with such open candour betrayed no nervousness or embarrassment whatsoever.

"And you accept?"

"I can hardly accept for someone else." Harriet smiled. "But, yes, you have my permission, and you will find Sarah delighted to see you." Harriet rose.

"Where are you going?" he asked, his voice sharp.

"Why, to fetch Miss Sarah."

"Do you need that chit's approval? You are the chaperone and not Sarah."

"But I am not a tyrant. I do not tell my charges whom they must marry!"

"Sit down," barked the marquess.

Harriet sat down again, her blue eyes filled with wonder.

"We appear to be talking at cross purposes. I shall make matters plain and simple. I wish to marry *you*, Miss Metcalf."

"Oh, no!" shrieked Harriet. "Not you as well!"

"Explain yourself."

"I thought Lord Vere had come to propose to Annabelle, but he proposed to me instead, And now you! I thought you wanted to marry Sarah."

"Why should I want to marry some chit barely out of the schoolroom?"

"She has a dowry," wailed Harriet.

"Money appears to control all your thoughts and motives. I do not want to marry Sarah Hayner. I want to marry you."

"I don't want to marry *you*," said the much-goaded Harriet.

"Why not?"

"I do not love you. You . . . you frighten me."

"I thought love did not enter into your calculations, my mercenary widgeon. I am rich—"

"I do not want money."

"I am a marquess."

"I do not want a title."

"Then, in heaven's name, what do you want?"

"I had not thought of marriage for myself," said Harriet. "Oh, but I should want someone to love me and cherish me and be faithful to me."

That was surely the marquess's cue to go down on one knee and swear undying love and devotion, but pride kept him where he was; pride made him say in a flat voice, "Then you ask the impossible. I once had all that to give and gave it to that heartless strumpet I made my first bride."

"I did not think you had ever been married," whispered Harriet.

"I am thirty-two."

"But with such a reputation for philandering—" began Harriet.

"Enough," he said. "I had forgot that tongue of yours. I must be out of my wits to have ever contemplated allying my name to a vulgar, countrified wench such as yourself."

"Oh, yes," agreed Harriet wholeheartedly. "So now you know I am not worthy of you, we may be comfortable again."

"Comfortable!" He seized his locks and gave them a massive pull. "Madam, pretend we have never met."

Once more, Number 67 saw the hurried departure of

a rejected lord. Once more, Annabelle and Sarah scurried upstairs to nurse their rage and burning cheeks.

"You see!" cried Annabelle. *"You see!"*

"I see," said Sarah. "Oh, here she comes. Tell her I have lain down with the headache and shall see her later."

Sarah gloomily listened to the whisperings at the bedroom door until Annabelle came back.

"And he *did* propose to her," said Sarah in a flat voice.

Annabelle nodded.

"She has done it again," said Sarah. "Anyone who might love us is ruthlessly snatched from us, and she stands there with her eyes full of tears, looking as if butter would not melt in her mouth, and says she had nothing to do with it. Isn't that the way of it?"

"She was sore distressed—or appeared so," said Annabelle. "But she did not accept him either."

Sarah rang the bell and when Emily appeared she said, "Fetch us champagne."

"I may wish you well, my ladies?" asked Emily.

"No, you may not wish us well," said Sarah. "We are in need of a restorative. Our dear godmother received proposals from our beaux all right, but they proposed to *her.*"

"I told you, ma'am," said Emily hotly. "She is not to be trusted."

"Get along with you," said Sarah wearily. When Emily had left, Sarah muttered, "I would like to kill Harriet."

"Why don't we get Emily to spread some gossip after all?" said Annabelle. "All we need to do is tell the truth. She did set out to steal Papa's affections away. She *did!*"

"Did she?" said Sarah. "Do you know, Sis, perhaps what makes Harriet such a formidable rival is that she never does mean any wrong. She did not do anything with Huntingdon and Vere other than run around trying to push them into our arms."

"But you said—"

"I said, I said," cried Sarah. "Do not let us discuss the matter further until we have had that champagne."

After Emily had left the servants' hall that night, the others sat in a stunned silence and discussed what the lady's maid had just told them about Miss Metcalf. "Emily was sore distressed, but I cannot credit it," said Mrs. Middleton. "That sweet Miss Metcalf should have been the mistress of Sir Benjamin Hayner, that she should be salting away the girls' fortune to feather her own nest!"

"Emily was certainly convincing," said Rainbird gloomily. "She practically choked it out in bits and pieces, and we had to drag most of it out of her."

"Them fair ones are always the most sly," said Joseph, who obscurely blamed Miss Metcalf for Lizzie's new coldness.

"I think that's awful rude of you, Joseph," said Alice, "seeing as how I'm fair meself."

"I hate Emily," burst out Lizzie, startling them all. "I've hated and distrusted her from the minute she arrived. She's the one what's sly. And if Miss Metcalf is such a low, selfish, and cunning woman, why then does she bother about a scullery maid's health or trouble to teach her her letters?"

"That's right," said Rainbird, "and I'll tell you something more. Seems to me as if Lord Vere and Lord Huntingdon was calling on Miss Metcalf, not on the Hayner girls and what's more got sent off. Now . . . let me think, Joseph, and I can't if you keep on strumming that mandolin. . . . What if the misses became jealous and told Emily to . . . ? Oh, it's nonsense. They would never do a thing like that."

"But we know her, we've spent a whole day with her," said Lizzie passionately. "Are we going to believe the evidence of our own minds and eyes and ears, or are we going to listen to that Emily?"

"The lassie's got the right o' it," said Angus MacGregor. "See here, it's no' Miss Metcalf that's done any wrong, and it's no' the Hayner girls, it's probably just that Emily is wanderin' in her head. We'll just be kind tae her an' no let on we dinnae believe her."

"And no repeating any of this to Luke or talking to the others at The Running Footman," said Rainbird sternly. "Emily's probably had one of these queer turns that take women sometimes. She'll be all right tomorrow."

Perhaps if Emily's gossip had found root in the servants' hall and had spread throughout the ton, Sarah and Annabelle might have been comforted by Harriet's humiliation. But as Harriet's popularity appeared to increase rather than decrease, so did their jealousy increase, and they disliked Harriet more than ever.

They dissembled well. Outside, they appeared much the same—giggling and laughing and flirting at balls and parties.

Sarah's anger was further fueled by two pieces of gossip. The Marquess of Huntingdon had gone back to his estates in the country and showed no signs of returning. Lord Vere had indicated in a drunken farewell to his friends that his heart was broken and had left to re-enlist in the army.

But lying in bed at night, Sarah often worried and wondered why Huntingdon could have preferred Harriet to herself. She was more modish than her godmother and certainly more beautiful.

But although the twins' vanity regarding their personal appearance was intact, they were still beginning to feel defeated. Each longed for a sphere where they could shine without the dampening presence of Harriet Metcalf.

Chapter Nine

When the Hymalayan peasant meets the he-bear in
　his pride,
He shouts to scare the monster who will often turn
　aside,
But the she-bear thus accosted rends the peasant
　tooth and nail
For the female of the species is more deadly than the
　male.

—Kipling

Miss Spencer was a great comfort to Harriet. She was often on hand to cheer her up and banish any guilt Harriet might feel because the two lords had proposed to her and not her goddaughters.

But as the marquess was still noticeably absent from ball or rout or opera or even from the opening dance of the Season at Almack's Assembly Rooms, Harriet's spirits began to droop again. She could not confide the reason to Josephine, for she was not very sure of the reason herself. It was only that Lord Huntingdon seemed like a sickness in her blood. She saw a tall man with chestnut hair at a ball, and her heart began to hammer against her ribs, but he turned round and revealed a raddled, aged, painted face.

But Miss Spencer, confident that all was well with Harriet and that her charges were behaving nicely, took herself off to the country for a few days, promising to make sure Harriet's cottage was aired.

After the opening at Almack's, Harriet's spirits sank even lower. She had a nagging pain at her temples and when, two days later, Annabelle and Sarah requested the carriage to make calls, she begged them to go alone and take Joseph to guard them.

It had been a blustery and chilly day. Harriet, lighting the candles in the back parlour, became aware of the time. It was getting on for seven o'clock, and the girls had not returned.

Then she heard the rumble of a carriage outside and ran through to the front parlour and looked out of the window. Her sigh of relief was cut short, for although Annabelle and Sarah descended, they looked up and saw her at the window and the unguarded look of dislike on both faces before they resumed their social masks made Harriet feel near to tears.

She did not go out to meet them. She could only be relieved when they went straight upstairs, calling for Emily. Harriet sat down wearily. The Season was turning out a disaster. She bitterly blamed Sir Benjamin. Now, looking back, she had to confess that he had been over-affectionate towards her compared to the cool way he treated his own daughters.

Joseph, who had been out with the twins, entered and handed her a note. "Someone must have pushed it through the letter box," he said. "It was lying on the hall floor as I came in."

"Thank you, Joseph," said Harriet. "It is no doubt some last-minute invitation." She carried the letter through to the back parlour and sat down to read it.

At first she could not believe her eyes. It was written in pencil in block letters.

"Miss Metcalf," she read, "If you do not want the Hayner ladies' reputation to be ruined, I suggest you see me this evening. I shall show you Proof that they are not the Legitimate Daughters of Sir Benjamin. Unless you wish me to broadcast this Proof, bring jewels with you and come to 10 Carrier Street, St. Giles. Do not tell anyone. I watch you and will know if you have." It was unsigned.

Harriet looked about her frantically. Her one thought was to get to the address. If the note turned out to be a farrago of lies, then she would be able to return and go to sleep. If it were true, then she must save the girls at all costs. For the first time, Harriet really began to wonder if she herself had unwittingly done Sarah and Annabelle a great deal of harm. The proposals she had received from Huntingdon and Lord Vere worried her conscience. Then she remembered she had heard that Sir Benjamin's wife had been vicious and flighty. All at once, it seemed to explain his preference for her company rather than that of his daughters. If they were not his own daughters, but he had honourably given them his name, it would explain everything. Harriet became terribly sure that the writer of the anonymous letter spoke nothing but the truth. She rang the bell.

Rainbird answered its summons. "Tell me," said Harriet, forcing herself to speak in a calm and steady voice, "where is St. Giles? I think I have heard tell of it."

"St. Giles is an evil place nicknamed by some The Rookery. It is the sink of London, a haunt of prostitutes and thieves."

Harriet took a deep breath. "But whereabouts is it? Oh, do not look so anxious. I am not going there. Say, for example, one left here on foot. . . ."

"It is simple enough. One goes up to Oxford Street, along Oxford Street until it becomes High Street, along High Street to Broad Street, and The Rookery is a maze of nasty streets on the left of Broad Street."

"Thank you," said Harriet faintly. "That will be all, Rainbird. You may take the rest of the evening off." Rainbird looked at her curiously, but the room was lit by only a few candles and her face was in the shadows.

He left and went down to the servants' hall and told Mrs. Middleton he was stepping round to The Running Footman. Rainbird was just turning the corner of Clarges Street when he saw Emily on the other side of Curzon Street, arm in arm with Luke. They were laughing and did not notice him. He thought no more about it at the time.

Back in the servants' hall, Lizzie was pleading to be allowed to go to church. Mrs. Middleton demurred. Lizzie was a Roman Catholic and went to St. Patrick's in Soho Square. The housekeeper did not like the idea of the young maid being out in the London streets unescorted, even though Lizzie had gone before and had come to no harm. At last, the housekeeper gave in, and Lizzie pulled her shawl about her head and shoulders and ran up the area steps.

Lizzie ran along Oxford Street because it was the best lit of all the roads she could take to Soho. The parish lamps had been fitted with new reflectors, and their flickering lights were magnified to give a little stronger light than their usual feeble gleam.

She was just about to turn down Charles Street, which led from Oxford Street to Soho Square, when she saw Miss Metcalf looking out of the window of a passing hack. There was something so agonised, so frightened about that face that Lizzie, without hardly a thought, turned and started to run after the hack.

When it entered Broad Street, Lizzie began to become worried. It was no place for a lady, no place for even such as herself.

The hack stopped at the corner of Broad Street and Diot Street. "You'll find Carrier Street up there, miss," called the jehu. "I ain't goin' farder and neither should you and that'll be h'extra for the dog."

Lizzie came running up just as Harriet was paying the fare. "Miss Metcalf!" she called.

Harriet turned a chalk-white face to Lizzie and hissed. "Go! Leave me this instant. You must not be seen with me. I command you to go."

Only a very old family retainer would have the courage to question her better's judgement. Lizzie bobbed a curtsy and turned and walked away. Beauty gave a disappointed whine.

Shoulders drooping, steps lagging, Lizzie looked around to see if she could see a respectable face, to see if she could see someone she could ask for advice. For surely Miss Metcalf would never come out of The Rookery alive.

And then she saw him, the Marquess of Huntingdon, driving his own travelling carriage, sitting up on the box. He was going slowly as if either his horses were tired or as if he had things on his mind.

Lizzie did not believe in coincidence. What other people might call a coincidence, Lizzie only saw as the hand of God. God had placed the marquess in the middle of Broad Street in front of her eyes. It was a Sign.

So Lizzie ran out into the road, calling shrilly, "My lord! My lord!"

The marquess looked down and saw Lizzie and stared at her in amazement and reined in his horses. "What are you doing here, girl?" he called down.

"Oh, please, my lord," called Lizzie, standing on tiptoe because he seemed so very far away up on the box, "it's the mistress. She's gone into The Rookery."

"The deuce!" The marquess threw the reins to the coachman, who was sitting next to him, and jumped lightly down.

"What is she doing there?" he demanded. "Which way has she gone?"

"I heard the driver direct her to Carrier Street."

"Give me the pistols, John," called the marquess to his coachman. Seizing the guns, he said to Lizzie, "You had better go home, young Lizzie."

"Let me come, sir, my lord," said Lizzie. "Miss Metcalf . . . Miss Metcalf is . . . has . . ." Poor Lizzie could not quite put into words what Harriet had done for her by considering her important enough to educate.

The marquess gave an impatient shrug and set off with long strides. It was uncanny, he kept thinking. He had been plagued by stronger and stronger thoughts of Harriet Metcalf the nearer he got to London. He had vowed he would never think of her again, she who had spurned his offer and driven poor Gilbert back to his regiment. And yet this waif had cropped up under his carriage wheels in the middle of the worst area of London to tell him that Harriet Metcalf had apparently lost her wits and gone into The Rookery. The Rookery was the camp of the lowest kind of vagrant and petty thief, the home of the wretch, male or female, who had sunk too low to be fit for ordinary loose company. They filled the old houses from garret to cellar, six or seven to a room. The streets, into which the sun could barely penetrate by day, reeked and fumed. All the streets twisted and turned and broke into little alleys, which again curled into each other in not one but a series of labyrinths. Strangers seldom ventured into them. Without knowledge, one could not find a way out, and to ask a direction was only to be sent farther in and, perhaps in some locked courtyard, to be seized by a group of hags and robbed.

The backyards of the tall old houses were piled high with litter, with stolen goods, and with all manner of offal. Sanitation existed only in the form of kennel and cesspool. At every corner was a gin shop. Some of the houses held schools for the training of young "prigs." Both girls and boys were trained as pickpockets and sent out to work the crowds.

As Lizzie and the marquess hurried along, above the nightly racket of The Rookery could be heard the screams of the children who had come home empty-handed receiving a whipping.

Harriet had found Carrier Street but could not find Number Ten, since the houses did not seem to have any numbers at all. She approached a group of women—if such red-eyed bunches of rags could be called women—and asked politely to be directed to Number 10.

"Yes, my lovely," said one who appeared to be the headwoman of the tribe. "Come along of us."

The women bunched around Harriet as their leader led the way down an evil-smelling alley. It was too foul-smelling even for Beauty, whose senses were stunned with all the rank odors. The alley was very dark.

"Where are we?" said Harriet nervously.

"Where you'll stay," whispered an evil voice in her ear. "Grab 'er."

A slimy hand was clamped over Harriet's mouth, and hands tore at her clothes.

Beauty, forgotten by the hags, leapt into action. In a flurry of teeth, his ruff raised, he snapped and bit. There were cries of alarm, and Harriet, finding her mouth freed, screamed for all she was worth. She clutched tightly onto her reticule that contained some of Sarah's jewelry. Sarah had been in Annabelle's room when she had taken it. Harriet had none of her own to bring.

In the dim alley, she could make out the gleam of eyes and hear the frustrated curses of her attackers as Beauty stood foursquare before his mistress and barked loudly—deep baying sounds which carried above the racket of The Rookery.

And then a shot was fired in the air. The eyes watching Harriet blinked and disappeared as the animals of The Rookery crept back into their holes.

"Miss Metcalf!"

Harriet recognized Lizzie's voice and shouted, "Lizzie! I am here!"

And then Lizzie was there, with a masculine figure looming behind her, a tall figure who drawled, "What in all that's holy are you doing here, Miss Metcalf?"

"Huntingdon!" gasped Harriet. "Sarah and Annabelle. The most dreadful thing . . ."

"Quiet," he said. "Come back to Broad Street and into the light before you talk. I have a brace of pistols with me, but in this blackness one of these fiends could creep up behind me and knock me on the head."

Sobbing with reaction and fright, Harriet allowed herself to be led out through a maze of alleys onto Broad Street. She wondered, despite all her worry and misery, how the marquess had managed to find his way back, not knowing that his sharp eyes had taken careful note of every turning on the way into the maze.

"Now, Miss Harriet," said the marquess.

Pulling that note from her reticule, Harriet gulped out her tale of the note. Strangely enough, she did not think of hiding its contents from him.

The marquess took the note from her and led her over to his carriage, where he leaned against the side and studied the letter by the light of the carriage lamps.

"My dear lady," he said, "you have been gulled. No one in The Rookery can write, or, if they can, not literate English like this. Someone has played a very nasty trick on you. Possibly the Hayner girls themselves. I suggest we return to Clarges Street with all speed."

In vain did Harriet try to protest that perhaps the grim evidence of their illegitimacy was probably in Carrier Street, and when she showed every sign of turning back and running into The Rookery, the marquess seized her round the waist and lifted her bodily into his carriage.

Harriet sat hunched in the corner, shivering with fear and misery. The flickering carriage lamp inside shone on her white face and large, tired eyes. The marquess, who was travelling inside with Lizzie and Harriet, found himself wondering who could have played such a vicious and dangerous trick.

When he helped Harriet down outside Number 67, he had to put an arm about her to support her, for when she looked up and saw that the only light in the house was coming from the kitchen, she swayed and seemed about to faint.

Lizzie made to go down the area steps, but the marquess said, "Come with us. Your mistress may need your help."

He raised his hand to knock at the door, but Rainbird opened it and stood back to let them past.

"Bring wine and . . . and something to the drawing room, Rainbird," said Harriet. "Are the Misses Hayner still awake?"

"Yes," said Rainbird. "Shall I tell them to come down?"

"No," said Harriet. "Wait for me, my lord. I shall return directly." She turned to the scullery maid. "Thank you, Lizzie. I have no further need of you. I shall see you, as usual, in the morning."

"Oh, mum," protested Lizzie, "there is no need for that. You'll be needing a long lie abed."

"No, Lizzie. Attend me as usual."

Rainbird, carrying an oil lamp, led the way up the stairs, dying of curiosity. What had happened? Why had Lizzie come home accompanied by the marquess and Miss Metcalf? Had Beauty misbehaved again?

Harriet went in to Sarah's room, which was at the front of the house. Annabelle and Sarah were both there and rose to meet her. The shutters were firmly closed and the curtains drawn, and the air was warm and overscented.

"That will be all, Rainbird," said Harriet firmly.

Rainbird bowed and withdrew. He could hardly wait to

get down to the servants' hall to find out from Lizzie what had happened.

Harriet moved slowly into the room and sat down wearily in a chair.

"What is the matter, Harriet dear?" cried Sarah. "You look so white."

"I received this letter," said Harriet. She handed it to them. The girls stood shoulder to shoulder as they read it.

"Gracious!" said Annabelle at last. "What nonsense! I trust you did not believe a word of it."

"I did not know what to do," said Harriet. "But I had to go. I could not risk doing anything else. I have no jewelry as you know. So I had to take some of yours. Do not worry, I have it safe."

"You did not go alone?" said Sarah.

"I took Beauty with me."

"But to venture into St. Giles!" exclaimed Sarah. "It is quite the wickedest part of London, and 'tis said that few strangers come back out alive."

Harriet sat very still. Then she said, "I had not heard of the place until this evening. How do you know of it, Sarah?"

"Someone was gossiping about it at some ball and said it ought to be burned to the ground," said Sarah.

"Who could have done such a thing?" asked Harriet. "What monster wishes me dead? I now know that any woman with a proper knowledge of London would never have gone there. But someone knew me very well. Someone knew that I would not stop to think clearly if I thought you were threatened."

"Why," said Annabelle, "did you believe such a piece of nonsense, you who have known us all our lives?"

"I have lately come more to realise," said Harriet quietly, "that Sir Benjamin perhaps did not appear to give you the fatherly love one might expect. I admired your father greatly. I could not help but think that were you not his natural daughters, it would explain his behaviour."

Sarah looked at Harriet, cold-eyed. "I should have thought your . . . er . . . attractions, my dear Harriet, were the obvious reason for Papa's coldness towards us. He preferred you and let everyone know it."

"You think *that!*" cried Harriet. "When you arrived home this evening and I saw the dislike in your faces when you saw me at the window, and then I received the letter, I began to think I knew the reason for that dislike. Oh, my dears, I have such love and concern for you. I would do anything to make you happy."

She held out her arms. The twins turned a little away, embarrassed by what they considered this vastly vulgar show of emotion.

Harriet let her hands drop helplessly to her sides. "You are not the ones who played such a trick on me by any chance?" she asked bleakly.

"Us!" squeaked Sarah and Annabelle in unison.

Sarah was the first to recover. "You claim to love us," she said icily, "and yet you are ready at the drop of a hat to believe us illegitimate, and now you think we deliberately tried to ruin you."

"Someone who knows me sent that letter," said Harriet. "But you are right. It is someone who knows the love I have for you both. And that is something you both do not know. I begin to see that both of you think I am an adventuress and opportunist."

A long embarrassing silence greeted this.

"But were you not attacked?" asked Sarah at last.

"Yes, I was. But Beauty fought off all comers." There was a scrabbling at the door as Beauty tried to get in. Harriet rose to her feet. "Beauty shall have the best bones from the kitchen. He is a brave and noble dog. Am I become such a creature in your eyes? Is Beauty the only one who can tolerate me?"

"You cannot have everything, dear godmother," said Sarah harshly. "You have control of our money until we are twenty-one. I suggest you comfort yourself with the thought if it were not for us you would still be languishing in that damp, pokey cottage of yours instead of being at the London Season and receiving proposals of marriage from two lords."

"I did not set out to win either of those gentlemen," cried Harriet. "Can you not see that?"

"I only see," said Annabelle, "that the hour is late. Strange as it may appear, we are glad you are unhurt. But please leave us."

They stood side by side and watched her. Now that Sarah had revealed their true feelings, neither twin could be bothered even to be polite to their godmother.

After Harriet had left, they looked at each other. "Well, now she knows," said Sarah defiantly. "And I don't care."

"Me neither," said Annabelle. But neither girl could quite understand why their cruelty to Harriet did not make them feel better, but only made them feel diminished in their own eyes.

Harriet hesitated outside the drawing room. She had not told the girls about Lord Huntingdon, for she had not wanted to upset Sarah, and she still felt guilty because the marquess had proposed to her, Harriet, and not to one of the twins.

The marquess was sitting with a glass of wine in his hand when she entered the room, and he stood up to greet her.

"I am grateful to you for this evening," said Harriet. She smiled. "And to my brave Beauty."

Beauty came and rested his head on her knee and gazed up at her with small, shrewd eyes. She patted his thick coat. He shook himself and then crossed over to the marquess, looking for more affection.

"Why," said the marquess, studying Harriet's woebegone face, "did you believe the contents of that ridiculous letter and go flying off alone to the worst part of London?

Surely you had no reason to believe the twins illegitimate."

Harriet wanted to tell him all about Sir Benjamin, and all about her guilt over his favoured treatment of her. But at the same time, she was afraid he might not understand. The patronage of the great man of the village, which seemed right and innocent in the country, took on a more sinister look in Town, where everyone seemed to credit everyone else with the worst of motives.

Instead, she said, "But what if it is true? What if someone does have such proof?"

"Then, my sweet widgeon," he said, "they meet you in Mayfair and probably with a lawyer in attendance. They do not tell you to come to The Rookery. Nor do they write letters in good English and push them through the letter box where they might be seen. Whoever delivered that note was confident that his or her appearance in Clarges Street would pass unremarked."

"I have received another shock this evening," said Harriet. "I fear Annabelle and Sarah dislike me."

"I did get that impression," he said dryly. "Are you sure *they* did not send that letter?"

"I am sure," said Harriet. "They may dislike me, but they would not wish my death."

"They might not have thought the adventure would kill you," he pointed out. "They might have thought merely to give you a fright. Spiteful people often do not pause to think of the consequences of their actions."

"I wish they did not dislike me," said Harriet. "Oh, it is distressing to find that two girls one has loved and cherished should nourish such feelings."

"Perhaps you should try to lavish your love on a more worthy object," said the marquess. "Just because two jealous misses do not like you, does not make you unlikeable. One must learn to accept lack of love just as much as love itself. Gilbert—Lord Vere—has left the country with his regiment," added the marquess abruptly.

129

"I am sorry," said Harriet, "but I could not marry him."

"Very few ladies have the privilege of turning down two handsome offers before the Season begins," he said.

"If I had known Lord Vere was going to take my refusal so hard, then I would have done all in my power to make amends to him," said Harriet.

"By marrying him?"

"No. Lord Vere is a romantic, and it would not be fair to saddle him with an unloving wife."

"But you would have been complacent had he proposed to one of your goddaughters?"

Harriet bit her lip. "Perhaps," she said. "I find the care of them onerous."

"And I am a beast to tease you so," he said. "Enough! Let us be friends, Harriet Metcalf. It seems that the gods will not allow us to stay apart."

"I should like that," said Harriet with such innocent surprise in her voice that he burst out laughing.

He rose and held out his hand. "Friends, then," he said.

"Friends," echoed Harriet, rising and taking his hand.

He smiled down at her. "I shall call on you tomorrow, Miss Metcalf," he said, "to see how you go on."

"Thank you," said Harriet, and the eyes that looked so trustingly up into his own were warm and affectionate.

He took his leave and dismissed his carriage, preferring to walk.

He felt quite lightheaded.

He could not remember being quite so ridiculously happy in his whole life.

Chapter
Ten

Who steals my purse steals trash; 'tis something,
  nothing;
'Twas mine, 'tis his, and has been slave to thou-
  sands;
But he that filches from me my good name
Robs me of that which not enriches him,
And makes me poor indeed.

—Shakespeare

The Marquess of Huntingdon was disappointed at not being able to see Harriet alone when he called at Number 67 the next day. Sarah and Annabelle were there, beribboned and beflounced, armed with portfolios of watercolours for him to admire and needlework to examine. He could only be thankful that Number 67 did not boast a pianoforte.

The girls were very arch, very coy, and asked him if he did not consider the house haunted, in view of its evil reputation. He said, no, he did not. They asked him if he had heard Brummell's latest witticism and he said he had, but they repeated it anyway and then giggled and slapped each other playfully with their fans. The marquess found himself becoming irritated with Harriet. Had she nothing to say for herself? Did she have to sit there with that fixed smile on her face while her charges bored him to death?

At last, he felt he could not bear any more of Sarah's and Annabelle's arch playfulness and took his leave. He felt quite happy, he told himself, that this silly schoolboy yearning of his for Harriet Metcalf appeared to have gone. She was nothing more than a soft marshmallow of a girl, whose only interests in life were her mongrel dog and her goddaughters. She was evidently determined to love two horrible girls who did not even like her. She was a martyr. And for such a one poor Gilbert was fighting battles under the hot sun in the Peninsula!

But by the time he had walked from Clarges Street to Berkeley Square, the old yearning for her was on him again. He knew she was to attend a ball at Almack's Assembly Rooms that evening. He disliked Almack's—a dreary place with a bad floor and worse refreshments. *He might,* he thought, *just look in for half an hour.*

Harriet now felt secure in society, secure enough to prepare for an evening at Almack's without any feelings of trepidation. She was ingenuously pleased with her new ensemble of a gown of silver embroidery on the sheerest mull worn over a slip of white satin.

Harriet was proud of herself. If only her treacherous mind would stop dwelling vulgarly on the physical perfections of Lord Huntingdon, then she felt she would be able to do her duty as a chaperone more wholeheartedly. At least she was a success in that regard.

Both Annabelle and Sarah had several very respectable beaux—none admittedly as dazzling as Lord Vere or Lord Huntingdon, but all young men of good family and sound fortune.

She herself was popular with the chaperones and had come to enjoy gossiping with them at balls and routs.

Sarah and Annabelle seemed to have decided it politic to treat Harriet as they usually did. They appeared moderately affectionate, but Harriet, with her eyes opened now to their real thoughts about her, felt she could have coped with honest and open dislike better.

Once in the ballroom, she waited until the twins had been led onto the floor by their partners and then walked over to the row of little gilt chairs, smiling as she recognised Baroness Villiers and Mrs. Cramp.

To her surprise, both ladies rose as they saw her approach, and without one word of greeting they walked away and stood together by the pillars under the musicians' gallery.

Puzzled and bewildered, Harriet sat down, conscious of the empty chairs on either side of her. She sent a timid smile along the row of chaperones, and they stared at her haughtily and then bent their heads towards each other and began talking in low whispers.

Nonplussed, Harriet turned her attention to the dance floor. More accusing eyes, more whispers.

She glanced down at her gown, fearing that her tapes had come undone or that there was a large stain on her dress.

And then she saw the fat and comfortable figure of Lady Phillips.

Determined to speak to at least one friend, Harriet hastened towards her.

"Lady Phillips . . ." she began, and then her voice trailed away. For Lady Phillips gave her one startled look, then her chubby features became a frozen blank and she turned on her heel and walked away. It was the cut direct.

Harriet retreated miserably to her chair. What on earth had happened?

When the Marquess of Huntingdon walked into the ballroom, Harriet looked across the room at him and sent him a tremulous smile. He smiled back and looked as if he were about to cross the floor to join her when he was hailed by two friends. They appeared to talk in low voices to him for quite some time, and then all looked straight at Harriet. The marquess was looking stunned.

He felt history was repeating itself. For was it not at Almack's that he first learned of his wife's infidelity? And had he not stood then as he was standing now with a wrenching pain at his heart and his world crashing down about his ears?

To think he had felt unworthy of her. To think he had thought her pure and chaste. The facts were damning. Why should Sir Benjamin Hayner set her up in control of his estates, fortune, and goddaughters, and she only a few years older than they? Evidently, it was well-known in the country that Harriet had set out to seduce him. He felt sickened.

As Harriet watched, he turned and began to talk to some other friends. And then he left the ballroom.

The whispers and stares became more marked. Harriet felt her eyes filling with tears and blinked them away. Illogically, she wished she had been able to bring Beauty, the only affectionate and stable thing in a treacherous world.

All at once, she could not bear it any longer. She stumbled to her feet, watched by hundreds of hard eyes. She scurried to the door, head bent, but all too aware that backs were turned and presented to her as she passed.

She collected her cloak and fled the Assembly Rooms.

From the other side of the street, the marquess who had been pacing up and down in a rage, saw her leave.

Let her go! he thought.

But as if joined to her by an invisible thread, he followed, quickening his pace as she plunged into the darkness of Chapel Court. Emerging from the court, she ran along New Burlington Street, Clifford Street, Grafton Street, down Hay Hill across the foot of Berkeley Square, along Bolton Row and into Clarges Street.

She was about to escape him, to plunge into that accursed house without giving him an explanation, thought the marquess, in too blind a rage to realise she owed him none.

Harriet was just opening the door of Number 67 when he caught up with her.

"A word with you, madam," he said.

Harriet said nothing, merely trailed into the drawing room, leaving the door open. He followed her in and waited while she lit the candles.

"I do not know what happened this evening. I could not bear it any longer," sobbed Harriet. "Those eyes and whispers and everyone cutting me dead."

"They do not care for harlots," he said in a cold voice.

She put a hand up to her cheek as if he had struck her. "What are they saying?" she asked, bewildered. "What have I done?"

"Your sins have found you out. The world now knows you were the mistress of Sir Benjamin Hayner and took away the love he owed his daughters. So clever were you he left his estates and fortune to you. . . ."

"Only the management of them until the girls are twenty-one," said Harriet, aghast. "And I am innocent, my lord. Sir Benjamin was like a father to me after my parents' death."

Perhaps if he had not wanted her so much, had not felt this desperate craving for her, he might have listened to reason. If his wife had not betrayed him, he would not have been so hot-headed.

"And to think I did not even dare to steal a kiss," he marvelled. He came towards her. Harriet backed away. He jerked her forward into his arms. He was going to jeer at her, punish her, but the feel of her body against his, the fear in the large eyes which gazed up into his own, filled him with a sort of aching tenderness. The glare left his eyes and the hard lines of his face softened. "Harriet," he said. "My very dear Harriet."

And the the world seemed to explode about them. Not with passion. . . .

Beauty had found the kitchen cat.

He had been lurking around the backstairs all day, watching as a cat watches a mouse hole, for an opportunity to get through the green baize door.

The opportunity was provided by Alice. Alice did everything so slowly that she took an age to open and shut a door. She had been clearing away the tea things for some time after the ladies had left for Almack's and, with the tray on one hip, she had nudged the door open with the other, with her usual lazy, languorous movements that Rainbird said were like watching someone walk under water.

Beauty saw his chance and took it. He leapt joyfully down the stairs and erupted into the servants' hall just as they were about to sit down for their evening meal.

He saw the Moocher, and his little bearlike eyes glowed red. With a snarl, he pounced . . . and then let out a yelp of pain. For the Moocher had stood his ground and slashed him across the nose.

Had Rainbird been there, order might have been restored more quickly, but Rainbird was at The Running Footman with Mr. Blenkinsop, the butler from next door.

MacGregor seized the rolling pin and ran at Beauty; Beauty feinted and bit Joseph on the leg. Joseph screeched like a parrot getting its tail feathers removed. Jenny jumped on the table, and Dave seized the Moocher and ran upstairs with Beauty, Mrs. Middleton, Lizzie, and Angus MacGregor in hot pursuit. Alice flattened herself against the wall as they all went roaring past.

Into the sanctuary of the drawing room ran the now terrified Beauty, forgetting about Dave, who was hiding in a corner of the hall with the cat.

Beauty stared at the sight of his mistress being held in the arms of some large and powerful human.

With a roar he took off and sank his teeth into the Marquess of Huntingdon's bottom.

The marquess swung around and lashed out at Beauty with his foot. Lizzie fell on Beauty's neck, crying, "Good dog. Be good. You *can* be good, Beauty," and other incoherent nonsense that had the amazing effect of calming the maddened animal.

The Marquess of Huntingdon looked on, appalled. He appeared as if he had been suddenly frozen to the spot. He could not believe what was happening to him. He, the arbiter of fashion, the Don Juan of the ton, the adored, the fêted and petted, was standing before a pack of goggling servants with a throbbing bum. Had it not been for the timely dog bite, then he might have been in danger of behaving very badly.

The attack from the wretched mongrel had cleared his brain wonderfully. He wondered if there might be insanity in his family. For he knew, deep down, that the gossip about Harriet Metcalf was a scurrilous lie. He wanted her as he had never wanted any woman before, and he began to think the longing was addling his brain.

A stillness fell on the servants. They looked at Harriet's anguished face and wondered whether they would have to throw this noble lord out of doors. Lizzie prayed for Rainbird's return.

And then all at once the butler was there, his face a correct blank. His eyes darted from one to the other and then he said politely, "I understand you are just leaving, my lord."

"Yes," said the marquess. He turned to Harriet. There was so much he wanted to say and yet the slow dawning fright and disgust on her face as she recovered from the stunning shock of his words drove it all from his mind.

"Your servant, Miss Metcalf," he said. "I shall call on you tomorrow to see how you go on."

And then he walked from the room as stiffly as a tom-cat giving up the fight.

Rainbird saw the tears spilling over onto Harriet's cheeks and jerked his head at the other servants. "Out!" he said.

They retreated and closed the door.

"I am only a servant, ma'am," said Rainbird, "but there is no one else here, and I cannot help you unless I know what troubles you."

In an instant, the class barriers were down. Harriet threw herself against his chest and sobbed her heart out.

Beauty threw back his head and began to howl, and the sound of her pet's distress had the effect of forcing Harriet to pull herself together. She stood back and surveyed the butler with sorrowful eyes. "I am being destroyed by malicious gossip, Mr. Rainbird."

"I know," said Rainbird gravely, "and I know who has been gossiping."

Harriet sat down abruptly and stared at him.

"It's that lady's maid, Emily. She told all to Luke and then swore him to silence. But he told his butler, Blenkinsop, as I am sure she must have known he would do. Blenkinsop loves a gossip and tattled to the upper servants at The Running Footman. I will say one thing for Luke," said Rainbird, studying his bruised knuckles, "he was very loyal to Emily and I had to . . . er . . . drag the source of his information out of him."

"But I have never done her any harm!" cried Harriet.

"I think you will find, Miss Metcalf," said Rainbird, studying the cornice, "that she was instructed to spread malice by the Misses Hayner."

"That I shall never believe," said Harriet.

Rainbird cocked his head to one side and listened as a carriage came to a stop outside.

"Prove us all wrong then, ma'am," he said. "Come with me and hide outside Miss Sarah's room when they have gone in, and listen."

"No!"

"If they are innocent, you have nothing to fear."

Harriet took a deep breath. "Very well."

Rainbird bowed. "I shall tell them you have retired to bed and are not to be disturbed."

He went out and closed the door. Harriet twisted her handkerchief in her hands and listened to the murmur of voices coming from the hall. Then she heard the girls mounting the stairs.

Rainbird slipped back into the front parlour. "Now, Miss Metcalf," he said.

Harriet followed him noiselessly upstairs. He signalled to her to press her ear against Sarah's door.

"Well, what a to-do!" came Sarah's voice. "I cannot understand it."

"It must be Emily," said Annabelle. "Or some of that gossip we had spread about Upper Marcham has finally come to Town."

"I wish you would not persist in calling it gossip," said Sarah testily. "We only spoke the truth and it was only our way of letting people *know* the truth."

Harriet shrank back from the door. "I have had a bad shock," she whispered. "I shall retire."

"Not yet," said Rainbird. "You did not listen long enough."

With a sick heart, Harriet put her ear to the door again.

"I thought you had come to like her," Annabelle was saying.

"I did . . . almost . . . when I thought she had our

interests at heart. Then I did think she might be sincere. But on calm reflection, I once more think she is a scheming jade. I hope she is so badly disgraced that no one will look at her again. Faugh! Harriet and her milkmaid manners and her lack of ton. She must be a schemer or the gentlemen would not look at her twice with us around. I do not like her one little bit. I never liked her. I never even liked her when we were children and before Papa showed any doting preference for her. . . ."

"Enough," said Harriet, backing away from the door.

"You must come to the servants' hall," said Rainbird gravely. "There is much work to be done."

Chapter
Eleven

Fair virgins blushed upon him; wedded dames
Bloomed also in less transitory hues;
For both commodities dwelt by the Thames,
The painting and the painted; youth, ceruse,
Against his heart preferred their usual claims,
Such as no gentleman can quite refuse;
Daughters admired his dress, and pious mothers
Inquired his income, and if he had brothers.

—Lord Bryon

Too shocked and dazed to do other than obey the butler, Harriet followed him down the backstairs and into the servants' hall.

The illogical thought did cross her mind that her poor mother would have been shocked could she have seen her daughter confiding in servants. And yet, for all her faults, for all her snobbery, the late Mrs. Metcalf had maintained that only upstarts and counter-jumpers treated their servants uncivilly.

Lizzie was sitting at the far end of the table, teaching Dave the little she had already learned from Harriet. Mrs. Middleton was nodding over a piece of sewing by the fire. Jenny and Alice had workbaskets full of linen to mend.

Angus MacGregor was standing on one foot, studying a much battered book of recipes; the book was held well out in front of him, for his eyes were bad and only vanity stopped him from buying a pair of spectacles. Joseph was manicuring his nails, and the Moocher was curled up on his knee. Candlelight shed a golden glow over the group around the table, shadowing the stained walls and making it look like an idealised painting of a country kitchen at the end of the day.

All rose to their feet as they saw Harriet behind Rainbird. Rainbird pulled out a chair at the head of the table and begged Harriet to sit down, and then nodded to the others to resume their places.

Mrs. Middleton was fully awake now, her mild eyes darting this way and that with a frightened look, for Mrs. Middleton, in her heart of hearts, really believed there was a curse on the house and wondered if Miss Metcalf had descended to these unfashionable lower regions to tell them of murder or rape.

Succinctly, Rainbird outlined the scurrilous gossip about Harriet that was spreading throughout the West End. He told them he now believed the twins had tricked Miss Metcalf into going into The Rookery. When all the exclamations of shock and dismay had died down, he turned to Harriet.

Harriet wanted to cry out that she did not believe the twins could have done such a thing, but Rainbird was asking her a question.

"Tell me, Miss Metcalf," said Rainbird, "I understand that Lord Vere and Lord Huntingdon both called on you some time ago and both gentlemen left looking distressed. Could it be that both proposed marriage to you?"

"Yes," said Harriet miserably. "I believed, you see, that Lord Vere wished to propose to Annabelle, and Sarah would receive a proposal from Lord Huntingdon. But they asked me instead."

"And you refused, obviously," cried Rainbird. "Did not Lord Vere talk of joining his old regiment because of a broken heart? But he never named the lady, and speculation was rife. And Huntingdon. Ah, there's a prize! Before he went to America, every society family wanted him for one of their daughters, and there were many married ladies who threw themselves at his head as well. But he never played any respectable lady false for all his reputation."

"Belinda Romney is his mistress," said Harriet. " 'Tis said she needed money badly after the death of her husband. He must have taken advantage of her."

"Not he," said Joseph. "She hehd two lovers afore him."

"You see," said Rainbird eagerly, "the only way to combat a nasty piece of gossip is to provide society with a bigger and better chunk. We shall spread out over the West End before morning and tell the world of the Hayner girls' jealousy and spite."

"It will ruin them," said Harriet miserably. "And their father trusted me."

"Sir Benjamin trusted you, Miss Metcalf, to see they remained ladies of good character. If they go unpunished, then they will remain malicious and go on to ruin someone else's life. Emily shall be sent packing first thing in the morning. I shall see her off on the stage myself. Now, what happened between you and Lord Huntingdon?"

"He spoke to me like the harlot he believed me to be," said Harriet.

"Well, it stands to reason he might be in a passion seeing that he obviously loves you very much."

"Loves me? The man is a rake!"

"Miss Metcalf," said Rainbird severely, "when a man as wealthy and handsome as the Marquess of Huntingdon proposes marriage, you must understand that man is deeply in love. His late wife played him false, you know, and he was very badly hurt by her."

143

Harriet looked at the butler with wide eyes. "Are we all talked about by London servants? Is there no part of our lives which is not taken apart?"

"Oh, yes," said Rainbird blithely. "But if we did not listen to gossip, how could we know all these things to tell you—to help you?"

"But no one will marry Sarah and Annabelle after you talk."

"Yes, they will," chipped in Jenny fiercely. "They've got large dowries. There's fellows would marry an ape, supposing it were wealthy."

"And by the look o' some o' the dowagers," chirped Dave, "it's obvious they did."

"No," said Harriet with a shake of her head. "I cannot believe the girls tried to get me to go to The Rookery. I cannot allow any gossip against them without proof."

"What more proof do we need?" asked Alice.

"I know," said Rainbird. "Jenny, fetch Emily down here. She's the one who's been spreading the gossip. I'll make her tell us why. I'm sorry, Miss Metcalf, but I am sure she will say she was under orders."

Mrs. Middleton roused herself from her transfixed state. "Brandy for Miss Metcalf, I think, Mr. Rainbird, while we wait for Emily."

A bottle of the best French brandy was produced. Harriet, feeling drained of emotion and oddly at peace, noticed that the brandy was not given only to her but to all the servants, even little Dave.

"It is now three in the morning," said Harriet. "You should all have been to bed this age."

"We always stay up until our betters have retired for the night," said Rainbird. "Ah, here is Emily."

The maid, looking furious, sat down at the table and glared at Rainbird. "What's the reason for sending *her* to pull me out o' my bed?" Then Emily saw Harriet, and a look of fear flashed into her eyes.

"Now," said Rainbird, "we have absolute proof, Emily, that you have been spreading nasty stories about Miss Metcalf. Did Miss Sarah and Miss Annabelle put you up to it?"

"I didn't spread lies," said Emily defiantly. "All I told was the truth. I did it all by meself."

"Do you realise what you are saying?" wondered Rainbird. "Not only will you now be dismissed, but you will never get another job again."

"Already got one," said Emily, tossing her head.

"With whom?"

"That's my business."

"Is it with that lady you was seen talking to in Shepherd Market?" asked Jenny suddenly. "Mary, the housemaid, what told me, said she had ever such green eyes."

"It come to me," said Lizzie excitedly, "the lady Beauty frightened off her horse, her what was with Lord Huntingdon, had green eyes."

"Belinda Romney," gasped Harriet.

"See here, young woman," said Rainbird, looming over Emily, "if Belinda Romney wrote that note to get Miss Metcalf to go to The Rookery, then you'd best tell us. If you won't talk to us, you'll talk to the Bow Street Runners."

"You wouldn't," said Emily, turning white. "They'd never listen to the likes o' me. They'd transport me. All she'd have to say is that she didn't know nothing about it."

"Then tell us," said Rainbird.

Thoroughly frightened now, Emily choked out her story. The girls often sent her out on errands. Mrs. Romney had fallen into conversation with her, asking her if she were the Misses Hayner's maid. She had seemed to have developed a knack of turning up when Emily was in some shop or bazaar. Emily loved to talk, and it appeared Mrs. Romney loved to listen. Mrs. Romney had said lightly that Harriet had stolen Lord Huntingdon away from her. Emily had poured out her version of Harriet and Sir Benjamin. One confidence led to another. Mrs. Romney had said it would be fun to worry Harriet by sending her a letter saying the twins were illegitimate. If Harriet swallowed such a story and went to The Rookery, she would only get a fright, and even if she did not go, it would worry her to know she had a secret enemy.

"Then when it didn't work, when it only brought Lord Huntingdon to her rescue," said Emily, her hands trembling, "Mrs. Romney grew angry with me and said if I had gossiped about her in the country, I could gossip about her in Town. My ladies did not want me to do it."

Harriet let out a slow breath of relief. Belinda Romney of the uncertain morals and cracked reputation was an enemy she could understand.

"She promised me twenty pound and a job if I did my part well," said Emily desperately. "Oh, Miss Metcalf, twenty pound is a lot of money for the likes of me." She buried her face in her hands and began to cry in earnest.

"I suggest you return to your home in Upper Marcham immediately," said Harriet. "I do not want to see you again."

Rainbird nodded to Jenny, who led the weeping and unresisting maid out.

"Now, let me see," said Rainbird. "We must move quickly to fight gossip with gossip. London must know of Mrs. Romney's spite and as soon as possible. Joseph, you will position yourself between White's and Brooks's in St. James's and gossip to the waiting grooms and footmen. Alice, you will go with Jenny; Miss Metcalf will lend you caps and cloaks so that you may both look like lady's maids. Go to Almack's in a hack and enquire after Miss Metcalf, affecting not to know she has left. Show shock and alarm. Go into the room where the ladies leave their wraps and gossip to everyone who will listen. MacGregor, you had best go to Boodles. It is, as you know, next door to White's and Brooks's, but Joseph will have his hands full. Talk to the coachmen and footmen. Mrs. Middleton, take Lizzie and go to Lady Bellamy's. Say you are looking for your mistress and find an excuse to gossip. She is having a ball, and some folk may have gone on there from Almack's. I, myself, shall go around the coffeehouses. Dave, you guard the house while we are all away. We shall all meet back here in an hour."

Dimly, Harriet felt she should protest, but matters appeared to have been taken out of her hands. Alice and Jenny followed her up to her bedchamber and selected caps and cloaks, giggling with excitement. Rainbird hovered impatiently in the doorway and then ordered Harriet to bed in an abstracted way, as if his temporary mistress were one of the maids.

Harriet lay in bed and heard the shufflings and bangs and bustles as the servants of Number 67 cheerfully set out on their gossiping campaign. How could she face the girls in the morning?

Now *she* disliked *them*. That they had gossiped about her to the village of Upper Marcham instead of telling her of their suspicions about her was too much finally to take. And in a way that knowledge hurt where knowledge of Belinda's spite could not. Harriet had turned down two of the best catches on the Marriage Mart, and all because of Sarah and Annabelle.

Before she fell asleep, Harriet came to the conclusion that Sir Benjamin Hayner had not liked his own daughters simply because they were unlikeable girls.

The Marquess of Huntingdon was engrossed in a quiet game of whist at Boodles. Boodles had a large bay window that commanded a good view of St. James's Street. Club history had it that a famous duke had enjoyed the prospect because he said he liked sitting "watching damned people get wet." It was a more soothing club than the politically minded Brooks's (Whig) and White's (Tory). It even boasted a "dirty room" where all coins were boiled and scrubbed so that they might not sully the hands of the gamblers.

The marquess glanced idly out of the window. Surely that was one was of the servants from Number 67! There was a large Highland-looking man with a shock of fiery hair, who was talking earnestly to a rapt audience of coachmen and footmen. The last time the marquess had seen him, MacGregor had been trying to catch Beauty. As he watched, one of the marquess's friends, Jimmy Fotheringay, drove up in his phaeton. He jumped down and eyed the listening group of servants and strolled over to them. He asked a question. The group parted to leave MacGregor in centre stage. With many wide gesticulations, the cook began to talk.

The marquess turned his attention back to the game. In ten minutes' time, Jimmy Fotheringay burst into the room, his eyes roaming this way and that until they settled on the marquess.

"Huntingdon!" he cried. "You have never heard such scandal!"

"Go away," said the marquess. "I have had enough of London scandal to last me until the end of my days."

"But this concerns the lady you proposed marriage to!"

The marquess's companions downed their cards and pricked up their ears.

"You forget yourself," said the marquess in an even voice.

"But she has been made the target of scurrilous gossip. That sweet angel has been pilloried by her two useless goddaughters and nigh killed by Mrs. Romney. You have never heard such villainy."

One of the card players, Lord Targarth, heaved his large bulk up from his chair. "Go away, Fotheringay," he said sleepily. "You never proposed to anyone, did you, Huntingdon?"

Had it been anyone less innocent and ingenuous than Jimmy Fotheringay, the marquess might have called them all to order and might have refused point blank to discuss his personal life. But affection for the ebullient Jimmy, combined with sudden sharp curiosity, made him say, "I proposed marriage to a certain Miss Metcalf. She refused me, and that's an end of it."

"But no, it isn't," cried Jimmy. Words tumbling out, he described the jealousy of the twins, the perfidy of the lady's maid, and the plot by Belinda Romney to have poor little Miss Metcalf permanently lost in The Rookery.

While more gentlemen crowded around to listen, the marquess sat very still, cursing his late wife for having poisoned his brain so much that he could no longer recognise goodness and virtue when he saw it. He remembered his behaviour and blushed for the first time in his life. He wanted to run from the club to Clarges Street, to rush into her bedroom and beg her forgiveness. Around him, the gossip grew in strength. The ladies left behind by their clubbable loved ones would have been amazed at the amount of gossip the flower of the masculine ton could bandy about.

Within another hour, Belinda Romney had hired assassins to kill Harriet in The Rookery and, mad with jealousy because Huntingdon preferred their godmother to themselves, Sarah and Annabelle had tried to poison her morning chocolate. Had not that cook said so? Had not he told them of his suspicions and fed a little of the chocolate to the kitchen cat? And was not that brave animal as stiff as a board some two minutes after lapping up the noxious mixture? MacGregor had said nothing of the sort, but when this tale emerged from inside the club to the ears of the servants outside, he considered it a very fine story indeed and said without a blink that it was all perfectly true. Tongues wagged and heads nodded.

149

At last, the marquess was able to persuade his friends to return to their game.

All hopes of wooing Harriet had fled. He had believed a thoroughly nasty piece of gossip as easily as any senile dowager. She would never forgive him. What lady would?

Sarah and Annabelle sensed something was wrong when Jenny rather than Emily appeared in answer to their ringing bells. Emily, said Jenny with flashing eyes, had been sent off. Longing to question Jenny and yet quelled by her hot, angry stare, the twins did not dare.

Looking out of the window later, Sarah saw bouquets of flowers and presents beginning to arrive. She let out a cry of excitement. "Our beaux have sent us gifts. Let us go downstairs. We had better ask Harriet why Emily is gone."

Harriet was sitting with Miss Spencer. Rainbird and Alice were carrying in more vases. Bouquets and parcels lay in heaps at Harriet's feet.

"You should have sent them up to us, Harriet dear," cooed Sarah.

"Why?" said Harriet harshly. "They are all for me."

"They cannot be," cried Annabelle. "Nobody likes you."

"Society has traced all the malicious gossip back to your maid," said Harriet, in a new, flat, hard voice. "It was Belinda Romney who contrived with Emily's help to get me to go to The Rookery. But it has come out that both of you had Emily spread gossip about me in Upper Marcham. How could you give a servant such power? It was enough to turn her head. How could you pretend to be so loving and so affectionate and hate me behind my back? Well, I don't like either of you anymore. Were it not for the affection and esteem I had for Sir Benjamin, I would leave you to your own devices. Go to your rooms and wait until I call you."

She rose to her feet, and the twins shrank back in the doorway, clutching each other.

"It's your own fault," shouted Sarah. "You took Papa's affection away from us. He preferred you to us . . . his own daughters. We *hate* you."

"I know," said Harriet calmly. "And I do not care. Go!"

She pointed to the door. Beauty advanced on the twins, his teeth bared.

With squeaks of alarm, they turned and fled.

"I must get out, Josephine," said Harriet. "The atmosphere of dislike in this house suffocates me."

"Then we shall go for a walk in the park," said Miss Spencer. "You must tell me everything again, Harriet, for I cannot quite take it in. But do leave that wretched animal behind. He looks even more evil than when I last saw him."

It was a grey, sad, misty morning with little drops of water dripping from the trees in the Green Park. Harriet and Miss Spencer walked as far as Buckingham House and then walked on into St. James's Park while Harriet told over and over again all that had been happening while Miss Spencer had been in the country.

"This Lord Huntingdon is indeed a monster!" cried Miss Spencer. "To say such things! Harriet, you must find a bed for me at Sixty-seven, for I shall make sure that man never approaches you again. *You* are the one in need of a chaperone."

Harriet's cheeks turned pink and she hung her head.

"Now, what have I said?" exclaimed Miss Spencer. "Harriet, never say you have formed a tendre for this brute."

"Josephine, there are things a lady should not discuss, things a lady should not even feel. I cannot explain," said Harriet.

"It is I, your friend, Josephine. There is nothing you could say about yourself that could shock me."

But Miss Spencer *was* shocked, and baffled, as Harriet quietly outlined the sick physical craving the very sight of the marquess aroused. The fires of passion had never burned brightly in Miss Spencer's chaste breast. Ladies surely never felt these passions. Men felt them—the brutes! Everyone knew that.

"Well," she said gruffly, "I shall move in with you just the same. Perhaps Harriet Metcalf needs a chaperone to protect her from Harriet Metcalf!"

Reluctant to return to Clarges Street and see the hate-filled eyes of her goddaughters, Harriet suggested they should repair to Gunter's in Berkeley Square for a refreshing ice. Over two hours had passed before Harriet's reluctant steps led her back to Number 67.

Sarah and Annabelle had left. A virulent note blaming Harriet for everything was all they had left behind. They had gone to stay, they said, with their aunt in Bath, where the fresh air and congenial company might help them forget Harriet's cruelty.

"So that's that," said Harriet wearily. "I had best return to Upper Marcham."

"Why?" demanded Miss Spencer. "The rent of this house is paid, you have these wonderful servants to support you. Dear Harriet, I have a comfortable income. I have always wanted an entrée into society. My relatives are gentry, as you know, but not of the first stare. I see on your mantel you have scores of invitations. Let me chaperone you, Harriet. We could have such fun," she added wistfully.

But Harriet was determined to return to her cottage, and only after a long argument with Miss Spencer did she give way and agree to stay for at least another week.

Harriet then had very little time to talk to Miss Spencer, for callers began to arrive in droves.

The Marquess of Huntingdon called at five o'clock to find Clarges Street blocked with carriages and Miss Metcalf besieged with well-wishers. He tried to convey to her his apologies, his regret for his behaviour, but he could not be very plain and open about it with so many listening ears.

Disappointed, he took his leave. Her eyes had changed, he thought sadly. They had lost that look of trusting innocence. She had looked up at him briefly as he had said farewell, and those blue eyes of hers had been mature, tired, and world-weary.

Chapter Twelve

Good-night to the Season!—Another
Will come, with its trifles and toys,
And hurry away, like its brother,
In sunshine, and odour, and noise.
Will it come with a rose or a brier?
Will it come with a blessing or curse?
Will its bonnets be lower or higher?
Will its morals be better or worse?
Will it find me grown thinner or fatter,
Or fonder of wrong or of right,
Or married—or buried?—no matter:
Good-night to the Season—good-night!

—Praed

After such a dramatic beginning to the Season, Harriet expected her hectic adventures to go on, but after a week, life settled down as much as it can settle down for anyone during the London Season.

The lawyer, Mr. Gladstone, wrote in reply to a letter from Harriet, expressing his shock over the twins' behaviour and strongly supporting Miss Spencer's idea that Harriet should stay and enjoy the Season herself. He said the

Hayner girls were well entrenched in Bath and surrounded by eligible beaux. He did not tell Harriet that they continued to revile her at every opportunity.

At first, Harriet was not able to enjoy any of it. She did not enjoy the novelty of being a celebrity and would have left for Upper Marcham had not society turned its frivolous mind to other things and other scandals and ceased to make her life a misery.

It was forcibly borne in on Harriet, however, that there were an amazing number of respectable gentlemen in society who did not seem in the least put out by her lack of dowry. Now that she had surrendered her place among the chaperones to Miss Spencer, she found she was never without a dance partner or escort.

Miss Spencer urged her to settle for some respectable gentleman of good fortune and so secure her future. But Harriet did not feel herself good enough to be the bride of any respectable gentleman. She craved the Marquess of Huntingdon's company. The longing for him was like a fever in her blood, and she dreamt many shocking dreams about him.

And yet there was nothing now in the marquess's behaviour to rouse mad passionate fancies in any female breast. He had raged at Belinda so much that she had moved out of Town until such time as she felt she could show her face again. She said she did not think Harriet would actually go into The Rookery, and the marquess did not know that the shrewd Emily had told Belinda that the naïve Harriet would probably rush there without thinking.

He was carefully polite and correct whenever he met Harriet at the opera or at a ball. He sometimes even, if rarely, asked her to dance, but always a country dance, one of the kind where one seemed to spend as much time dancing with other gentlemen in the set as one did with one's own partner. He did not ask her to waltz. The fact that he did not ask anyone else was small consolation to the tor-

mented Harriet, who longed to feel his hand at her wais
and then harried herself with introspection over her un
ladylike lusts.

She had been uneasy about the servants immediately
after the twins' departure—for surely her behaviour had
given the staff licence to be familiar? And had she not
blamed the twins for giving a servant power by taking her
into their confidence? But all were correct to a fault and
treated her with great respect.

Every morning, she continued to school Lizzie and
took delight in the scullery maid's enthusiasm for her
books.

At first, the end of the Season seemed a long time
away. Then all at once it came rushing upon her in a flurry
of hectic balls, routs, and picnics. Five respectable gentlemen proposed. Five were given Miss Spencer's permission
to pay their addresses to Harriet, and all five were disappointed when the fair Miss Metcalf sadly refused all their
offers.

"What do you want in a husband?" cried the much
outraged Miss Spencer. But Harriet could no longer bring
herself to confide her strong feelings for the marquess to
her friend.

Meanwhile, the marquess received a long letter from
Lord Vere. It was full of enthusiastic descriptions of battles.
He added he was grateful to sweet Harriet Metcalf for having been the means of removing him from the boring London scene.

The marquess studied the letter thoughtfully. He had
often wondered if courting Harriet Metcalf might be unfair
to poor Gilbert, who had appeared to suffer so badly because of her rejection of him.

The end of the Season was very near, the marquess
realised, a Season during which he had done nothing but
ache and long for Harriet Metcalf. He wanted to ask her to
go driving with him, and yet he was frightened to be alone

with her in case he found she had nothing but contempt for him. After all, it was his mistress who had nearly caused her harm.

He called at Number 67 only when he knew there would be other callers there. He watched Harriet when he was sure her attention was engaged with someone else, studying the shine of her hair, the soft femininity of her figure, and the dainty turn of her wrist.

Only Rainbird, serving biscuits and wine, turned one afternoon and surprised a look of longing in the marquess's eyes.

Miss Metcalf's financial circumstances were well-known to the servants. They could not understand why she did not want to marry any of the solid and worthy suitors who had tried to claim her hand in marriage.

Rainbird found excuses to busy himself about the front parlour until the Marquess of Huntingdon took his leave. He saw the carefully guarded look in Harriet's eyes as she curtsied good-bye to him, and then noticed that all animation seemed to have gone out of her after he had left.

That evening, when Harriet and Miss Spencer had gone to a rout at the Bellamys' in Curzon Street and had sent Joseph back, telling him to call for them in one hour, Rainbird gathered all the servants together and outlined the problem. Miss Metcalf was in love with the Marquess of Huntingdon. The marquess was in love with Miss Metcalf, but obviously they were never going to get together because of the Awkwardness created by the marquess's rough behaviour on the night he had believed Miss Metcalf to be a tart.

So, said Rainbird, it obviously followed they must do something about it.

"Och, it's a peety we cannae just throw them in a bed together and lock the door," said Angus MacGregor.

"Don't be vulgar," snapped Rainbird, noticing the shocked look on Mrs. Middleton's face.

"Why bother?" drawled Joseph. "She'll soon be gone and that'll put an end to Some People getting ideas above their station." He sent a smouldering look in Lizzie's direction, noticing to his fury that her eyes no longer filled with tears when he teased her.

"Why bother, you man-milliner?" said Jenny. " 'Cos she's given us good wages and been sweet and kind and gentle, which is something the likes of you, Joseph, would know nothing about."

"Squabbling isn't solving this problem," said Rainbird impatiently. "Even that wretched dog has become as quiet as a lamb. You overfeed him, Angus. All he does is sleep. Why doesn't he bite Lord Huntingdon and she could throw herself into his arms, or bathe the wound?"

"Not if he got another one on his bum," said the cook with a great horse laugh.

Mrs. Middleton was a great believer in the power of love letters.

"Why do we not send him a letter—a very . . . hmm . . . warm letter supposed to come from Miss Metcalf—and ask him to call, let me see, tomorrow at ten in the evening. She will be returned from the Franklyns' rout and will not be going on to the Phillips' musicale until midnight."

"Even if that worked," said Rainbird, "what about Miss Spencer? How would we get rid of her?"

"Tie her up," said Dave gleefully.

"Miss Spencer is very fond of Mr. Rainbird," said Lizzie. "We could get her down here and keep her here for a bit. Awfully fond of a good bottle of wine is Miss Spencer."

"But Miss Metcalf would wonder at you taking Miss Spencer off," pointed out Alice, "and her might come down here to see what was going on. Then when his lordship arrived Miss Spencer would go upstairs as well."

"I think I could arrange to see Miss Spencer quietly," said Rainbird with a mocking twinkle in his eye. "Look, it is not a very strong plan, but unless we can think of anything else, we had better try it."

They sat up late, mulling over first one plan and then the other. At last they settled for Mrs. Middleton's idea. Rainbird darted up the stairs to collect good quality parchment and the plain seal Harriet used for her letters.

Mrs. Middleton drew the candle nearer her and began to write. She imagined she was writing to Rainbird and the flowery effusion she produced received warm praise.

"My dear Huntingdon," Mrs. Middleton had written, "I am shortly to leave for the Country and do not wish to go without saying good-bye to One whom I have forgiven long ago, to One whom I think of daily. If my tender words do not disgust you, if you should wish to receive the warm tokens of my Esteem, if you would grant me Licence to bid you a tender farewell, please present yourself here at ten of the evening. Yr. Humble and Obedient Servant, H. Metcalf."

"Lovely!" said Rainbird. "Joseph may deliver this first thing in the morning."

"Read it out," urged Dave.

The butler read it out; the ladies sighed, but the cook said, "He will know it didnae come from her. It lacks elegance."

Mrs. Middleton looked as miserable as a poet who had just been savaged in the *Edinburgh Review.* The others leapt to her defence, and Angus was told to go and put his head in one of his cooking pots.

In the morning, Rainbird, being assured by Jenny that Miss Spencer was up and dressed, scratched at her bedroom door. Rainbird was the only man who had ever appeared on Josephine Spencer's horizon to make her sometimes regret her spinster state. She liked his sparkling grey eyes and his comedian's face. She liked his wiry body. She liked the way the butler, without stepping one inch out of line, made her feel like an interesting and attractive lady. So when Rainbird asked her if she would come to the servants' hall at quarter to ten that evening so that he might ask her sage advice about a personal matter, she readily agreed. When he added that he would rather she did not mention the matter to Miss Metcalf, for although Miss Metcalf was a sterling lady, she did not possess Miss Spencer's knowledge of the world, Miss Spencer, much intrigued, promised not to tell Harriet.

Dressed in his best livery, Joseph presented the forged letter at the marquess's town house. Angus MacGregor was right. The marquess did not believe it came from Harriet at all and wondered if Belinda were back in London and plotting mischief. He was about to send it to her with a covering letter, explaining his suspicions, when he thought it might after all be an excuse to see her alone. He knew she was leaving London, and he could not bear the idea of her going without at least having a short word with her in private. The letter would provide a good excuse. He would pretend to believe she had actually written it. As the day went on, the longing to believe she had actually written it overcame his common-sense and as the hour of ten approached, he found he was dithering like a schoolboy, throwing away one mangled cravat after the other until he achieved the desired effect.

Miss Spencer was at first put out to find the servants' hall full of servants. But Rainbird ushered her up to the housekeeper's parlour on the half-landing of the backstairs, saying Mrs. Middleton had kindly agreed to let them have the use of her room.

The other servants had strict instructions to leave the house as soon as the marquess had been ushered in. Joseph was to be sure to take Beauty with him.

By five to ten, Rainbird had Miss Spencer's full attention. With a glass of fine claret in her hand, she listened to all the tales of adventure and mayhem that had happened at Number 67. What the butler wanted her advice about, he would no doubt get around to soon. But meanwhile, it was pleasant to sit in the cosy parlour and listen to this amusing and attractive butler. She should be leaving soon, but Harriet would ring the bell in the front parlour and ask for her presence. Miss Spencer settled back to enjoy herself.

The marquess found himself received by Joseph and ushered into the front parlour. Joseph bowed and said he would fetch Miss Metcalf.

He met Harriet on the stairs. She had changed her gown and started in surprise when Joseph said the Marquess of Huntingdon was waiting to speak to her.

"Miss Spencer is there, I trust?" said Harriet.

"Yes," said Joseph, reflecting it wasn't really a lie because Miss Spencer was there in the housekeeper's parlour and Miss Metcalf had not asked if Miss Spencer was in the front parlour.

Then Joseph ran downstairs and joined the others. Like a little army on the move, they all crept up the area steps, Beauty silenced by a large bone between his jaws, and made their way silently off into the night.

"My lord!" exclaimed Harriet when she saw the marquess was alone. "Pray be seated while I fetch Miss Spencer."

Harriet rang the bell beside the fireplace. Rainbird had cut the bell wires in the kitchen so that there would be no jangling noises to make Miss Spencer suspicious.

"She will be here presently," said Harriet, chiding herself for being so nervous. After all, the house was full of servants.

"I came," said the marquess, standing up again and beginning to pace up and down, "because I received this odd letter supposed to come from you."

He turned and held it out.

Harriet read it carefully. "No," she said. "I never wrote it."

He felt quite flat and miserable.

"Nonetheless, Miss Metcalf, I am here, and it is the first time I have seen you alone and so I wish to apologise, most sincerely and with all my heart for having attacked you so brutally. Although I did not write that letter, it expresses —rather badly—my own sentiments. I could not bear to see you go without saying farewell."

"I had forgiven you a long time ago," said Harriet, twisting her hands in her thin muslin gown. She had little blue flowers twined in her hair and looked so virginal and at the same time so very seductive that he realised he must leave quickly before he forgot himself.

"Miss Metcalf," he said, "I once proposed to you. I found you . . . attractive . . . more attractive than any lady I have ever known. But I was merely grabbing at you like a spoilt child will grab at sweets. Have no fear that I will press my unwelcome attentions on you again. You are honesty and purity itself, and you are too good to be tied to the likes of me."

"You do yourself an injustice, sir," said Harriet.

"It is you, and you alone, who makes me feel like a slavering monster."

Harriet's kind heart was touched.

"I do not think you a monster," she said gently. She stood on tiptoe to kiss him on the cheek, moved by a mixture of longing and compassion. But as she made to kiss his cheek, he twisted his head in surprise, and the kiss landed full on his mouth. He desperately tried to control himself, but his arms went around her like steel bands, and he buried his mouth deep in hers, kissing her desperately, pulling that soft pliant body tight against his own. Caught up in his own dizzying and roaring passion, he was unaware that the once chaste lips under his own were parting, that the body against his was pulsating and throbbing.

With a sudden cry he broke free. "Forgive me!" he cried and strode to the door.

162

"Huntingdon!" shrieked Harriet, catching at his sleeve. "You cannot leave me. Kiss me again."

He picked her up in his arms. His face swam before her own before his mouth came down on hers again and one long hand came round to close over her breast.

"Harriet!" Miss Spencer jumped to her feet. "I heard Harriet cry out."

"It was someone in the street, my little love," said Rainbird.

Miss Spencer stood and looked at him open-mouthed, wondering whether she had heard the endearment or had just imagined it. Rainbird sent up a prayer to the god of love to give him courage. All he needed was the strength to last the next half hour. Surely by that time the couple upstairs would have got around to resolving something.

"I am a humble servant, Miss Spencer. I am married," lied Rainbird. "My poor wife lives in the country, and although I do not love her, I cannot desert her."

"But servants cannot marry," said Miss Spencer.

"I married very young, before I came into service," Rainbird went on. "I knew you were leaving soon and . . . and . . . I wished a little of your company. If you are disgusted by my presumption, please leave."

"Oh, Rainbird." Miss Spencer sighed, moving towards him, her arms outstretched. "How could I leave you now?"

"I can never leave you, Harriet," the marquess was saying. "I do not wish to frighten you with my lovemaking, but you must marry me."

Harriet buried her face in his chest and said shyly, "Oh, Huntingdon, the force of my feelings for you frightens me!"

The besotted marquess kissed her again, and again, and again.

Somehow, they descended to the floor, their mouths

still locked. And then after kissing her practically senseless, the marquess rose on one elbow to gaze down fondly on his beloved's face, and that was when Harriet felt a gentle breeze from the window moving across her bared breast.

"We are quite mad," she said, sitting up and hitching her gown onto her shoulders again.

"Josephine will be here any moment."

"We will be married soon?" he said.

"Yes," said Harriet. "Very soon."

He stood up and lifted her to her feet and tenderly helped her to straighten her ruffled hair.

"Then we shall be respectable till then," he said. He listened to the abnormal silence of the house, and then he laughed.

"I know who wrote that letter, my sweeting. You have the best servants in the world."

"Perhaps Josephine—Miss Spencer . . . ?"

"No, she disapproves of men such as I, and she would disapprove of you, my sweet, if she could see your abandon!"

The servants of Clarges Street sat out under the stars in the Green Park and wondered how Rainbird was faring and whether their plan had worked. Beauty lay snoring with his head on Lizzie's lap.

"It has been a lovely Season," said Lizzie softly. "I feel different. It makes you feel different, being educated. I can read most of the newspaper now."

"You'll be going off and leaving us," said Joseph. "And who cares? Not me anyhow."

Lizzie smiled a little smile and leaned forward and put her hand over Joseph's. He covered her hand with his other hand and glared up at the stars. He looked very angry, but he did not release her hand.

"D'ye think we'll ever get our freedom?" sighed Alice. "Me and Jenny had ever such a nice pair of fellers interested in us at Brighton. But they was soldiers with no money, nohow, so how's they going to keep us? Not that they even mentioned marriage. Still, it would be rare to be able to walk out with a handsome chap, don't you reckon, Jenny?"

"Well, one of yis can marry me when we get our pub," said Angus MacGregor, and that sent them all into gales of laughter, particularly when Angus said he would settle for any of them.

"Mr. Rainbird says another Season like this 'un, and we'll be well on the way to getting that pub," said Dave. "What'll we call it?"

They all settled down to their favourite discussion—naming the pub—while back at Number 67, Rainbird strove manfully to keep Miss Spencer occupied, and the Marquess of Huntingdon kept trying to tell himself he could leave after one more kiss . . . and another . . . and another.

The end of the Season. Miss Spencer was the first to leave. Harriet was leaving later in the day to stay with the marquess's parents, the Duke and Duchess of Parveter.

Harriet and the servants stood outside on the step to wave good-bye to Miss Spencer.

Miss Spencer gave Harriet a hug, then she shook hands with the servants in a mannish way, and then she turned to the butler.

"Good-bye, Rainbird," she said. Her eyes had a warm glow, and her leathery face softened as she looked at him. "Thank you . . . oh, thank you for everything."

Rainbird looked at her, turned a little away from the other servants, and to her amazement, Harriet saw one of his eyelids droop in a wink.

Then in the afternoon it was Harriet's turn to go. She had tried to take Lizzie with her, promising her the post of lady's maid, but with many tears Lizzie had refused. She knew the others would stay together, and she wanted to be with them when they all managed to gain their freedom.

They were flattered and delighted to receive not only a purse of sovereigns from the marquess but a warm handshake all round. Harriet was handed into the carriage with Beauty, who was chewing up shreds of silk after having torn off the ribbon Harriet had placed about his neck. The marquess stood with one foot on the steps, looking at the servants all lined up. His eyes moved from one face to another and then came to rest on that of Mrs. Middleton.

"An excellent letter, Mrs. Middleton," he said. "You certainly put your heart into it."

Mrs. Middleton let out a surprisingly girlish giggle and buried her face in her hands.

The carriage turned the corner into Piccadilly. They waved until it had completely disappeared and then trailed into the house, feeling let down and dejectd.

There were beds to be aired and covers to be brought out and furniture to be shrouded.

And then there were the old prayers to be said, the ones they said at the end of every Season.

"Thank you, Lord, for this Season's tenant. Please send us a tenant for the next."